# SHORTS

*Vida Cody*

First published 2023

Copyright © Vida Cody 2023

The right of Vida Cody to be identified as the author of this work has been asserted in accordance with the Copyright, Designs & Patents Act 1988.

All rights reserved. No part of this book may be reproduced, stored in a retrieval system, or transmitted in any form or by any means, electronic, electrostatic, magnetic tape, mechanical, photocopying, recording or otherwise, without the written permission of the copyright holder.

This is a work of fiction. Any similarity to actual persons, living or dead, or actual events, is purely coincidental and not intended by the author.

Published under licence by Brown Dog Books and
The Self-Publishing Partnership Ltd, 10b Greenway Farm, Bath Rd, Wick, nr. Bath BS30 5RL

www.selfpublishingpartnership.co.uk

ISBN printed book: 978-1-83952-690-9
ISBN e-book: 978-1-83952-691-6

Cover design by Andrew Prescott
Internal design by Andrew Easton

Printed and bound in the UK

This book is printed on FSC® certified paper

# SHORTS
## Tales worth boiling the kettle for

# VIDA CODY

*For Mum, Dad and Tia*
*For their love and unwavering belief in me*

# CONTENTS

| | |
|---|---:|
| A Bee in One's Bonnet | 9 |
| The Wee Small Hours | 13 |
| Giving Up | 16 |
| The DIY! Customer | 20 |
| Junior | 24 |
| A Guinea Pig Under the Shed | 28 |
| Kathleen Contemplates | 31 |
| Gooseberry Fool | 35 |
| Estelle and Ezekiel | 40 |
| The Letter | 42 |
| When the Future Comes Early | 46 |
| Couch to 5k | 50 |
| The Art Class | 54 |
| The Puzzle | 58 |
| A Home of their Own | 62 |
| To Have and To Hoard | 66 |
| Different Perspectives | 69 |
| The Grass is Always Greener | 76 |
| Getting to Know You | 80 |
| Decluttering | 86 |
| The Cemetery | 90 |

| | |
|---|---:|
| The Suet Ball Challenge | 94 |
| Pendle, Lancashire | 99 |
| The Freebies | 103 |
| The Seed | 108 |
| Tears of a Clown | 114 |
| A Game of Skittles | 118 |
| The Homing Pigeon | 122 |
| Silent Night | 127 |
| Shorts | 132 |

# A BEE IN ONE'S BONNET

Lady Primbold had often thought about keeping bees. A skep or two of one's own would look lovely in the garden, especially on a summer's day when the sun was shining and the bees were at their work. She had a somewhat romantic picture of herself in her white suit and veil, extracting the honey fresh from the hive ready for bottling and selling on. There she would sit, labelling jars from the comfort of her spacious kitchen, keeping some to one side as presents. The thought never occurred how messy this might be or how sticky her surfaces would become. Nor did she think she might be stung or her bees might swarm when seeking pastures new. Lady Primbold never thought much at all, though she had her opinions and forthright views.

She also liked to organise things, people mainly if given the chance. A staunch member of the parish council, she was rather formidable when holding forth, on every topic from summer fetes to burials. The graveyard was very full already and outsiders from the village were just not welcome. There was - what she'd call - standing room only and that kind of caper only happened abroad when they'd run out of room in those high-rise tombs. She'd seen it herself when visiting Spain, seen how the families would climb to the top, to place their jars of bright red flowers, wilting in the late summer heat. It was most unseemly and foreign and out of place in an English country village.

The parish council was due to meet and already had Lady Primbold's attention. Item six had caught her eye and some had seen her patrolling the village, making notes and taking photos. She'd complained about the parking before, many times, to anyone who'd listen and mostly to those who most definitely would not. If this was the way of the world these days, with every inhabitant wanting a car, the village would soon be overrun and would fast resemble a parking lot. To Lady Primbold, it did already and something simply had to be done.

Lady Primbold owned a car, kept in her garage and seldom used. She rarely left the village these days and took the bus if she ever did, some had said to prove her point – that cars were not in fact needed at all and half the time were status symbols, the bigger the better to show off your wealth.

Lady Primbold's car was small, in contrast to her many riches, gained from her husband's business interests and from being born herself into an upper-class family. She wasn't one to flaunt her wealth and readily gave to those in need, quietly, with minimum fuss.

Striding out through the village, Lady Primbold counted the cars. Far too many for a small population, numbers too great for a village this size. Barely a foot of space between them, parked on corners and over her drive. Some at odd angles, some jutting out, impeding the progress on road and path. Lady Primbold watched young mothers, pushing prams round oversized cars, half on the pavement and blocking their journey, forced continually to weave in and out.

Anger mounting, she marched down the street, her blood pressure rising with every step. How was the bus supposed to get down here when the bus stop itself was jammed with cars? No one else seemed to notice such things, no one else seemed even to care. So many times, she'd made her voice heard - at the council meetings, four times a year. Here it was on the agenda once more, at her own request, yet again.

Rancour burned deep inside her as she thought of those with several cars. Surely five weren't really needed, especially when they worked from home! There really ought to be a policy of how many cars a family could have. Space was certainly at a premium and selfishness should be disallowed.

Inching his way down the street, no pull-in place to help him out, a delivery driver lost his patience, shouting obscenities from his cab. Lady Primbold flagged him down, asking that he hush his voice. Children lived in this small village and language like his should not be heard. If she could but get him on her side, raise an army of like-minded people, she might just yet have a fighting chance when the parish meeting came around.

So long had she fought this village war, she ought by now to be battle weary, but Lady Primbold soldiered on, mustering troops as she went. She next engaged a handful of staff from the ambulance station down the way, fed up – like the delivery man – of having to force their way down the street, frightened of causing more of an accident than the one they'd originally come to attend to.

General Primbold, as she'd come to be known, won her case at the council meeting, her colleagues beaten down at last. A car park was built behind the old mill house, on disused land and out of sight. The villagers had but steps to walk and the street itself was vehicle free, save for those who were passing through and those who came on a mercy mission. Primbold looked out at her beautiful village, a rural idyll and delight once more, the battle finally won. The bees would lie dormant for now.

# THE WEE SMALL HOURS

If only she didn't like cheese, Minnie thought to herself as she tossed and turned in bed that night, her tired eyes and aching limbs fighting to capture a well-earned sleep. There were other produce that kept you awake, like chocolate, a late-night coffee or too much alcohol but cheese, Minnie knew, was her personal failing and rather too much of it had been consumed that night.

It was close to Christmas and the shops were just full of exciting cheeses, home-crafted and foreign, semi-soft and hard, cheddars and blue vein, tempting the taste buds of this self-confessed addict. Arriving home late after a busy day's shopping, too exhausted to prepare a regular meal, Minnie had opted to start on her cheeseboard, unwrapping the packets with undisguised love, carefully placing each piece on a round, wooden board in eager anticipation of a cheese fest for one.

Having given up early on the pretence of a proper cheese knife, Minnie sat hacking wedge after wedge, trying each one in turn and savouring every mouthful, delighting in the choices she'd made. She should have bought more of that soft Italian, so smooth and creamy and light on the tongue. So hard to resist its blue-veined charms, she kept on cutting till there remained not a crumb.

She hadn't intended to eat so much but eat it she had and now cursed her greed as she stared at the ceiling from her sweat-soaked bed. She picked up a book and tried to read before throwing it down on the floor beside her, eyes too sore from following the lines. She hadn't liked the book anyway, a bad translation from a Portuguese text, too literal by far in interpretation with a plot so obscure it addled the brain. Another one for the charity shop.

Oh why could she not sleep? Others managed it all the time like her ex who could sleep on a very bent pin and her cat who curled in a ball and was off. So easy for those who didn't like cheese, so hard indeed for those who did.

Stretching her legs, Minnie got cramp, another agent to keep her awake, taunting her with unbearable pain as her calves tightened into a round, hard mass. Up she got, to straighten her legs, treading hard on the floor to release the muscles, yelping with pain as she did so. Tonic water, she had read, was good for cramp although she would much sooner have the gin that went with it. *Mother's ruin*, they called it, although it had never done her any harm and on many an occasion had done her good. A little of what you fancy…

Now she was up, she pottered downstairs, filling the kettle for a cup of tea. Flicking the switch, she gazed out the window, watching a fox crossing the lawn. On velvet paws he silently moved, unaware he was being watched until a sudden movement from inside the house startled him and made him flee. Minnie wished she had stayed standing still, with something to look at while the kettle boiled. Unsure that she wanted tea anyway, she left the room and went back upstairs, leaving the fox to return for his food. How sad to be a nocturnal animal, awake at night while others slept. So thought Minnie as she climbed into bed, a worthy companion for the now active fox.

# GIVING UP

Dry January. It had been nothing like that. It hadn't stopped raining for one thing and Cathy hadn't stopped drinking, for another. People today seemed obsessed with their health and with keeping fit. Dry January was a fairly recent notion that pandered to that. In theory, it was a good idea, Cathy thought, but how many people stuck to it and how much had they drunk in December that made teetotalism a real necessity? Previous generations had managed perfectly well without all this dry malarkey and, with a few exceptions, had hung on to a healthy liver well into their old age. Moderation was the key to everything, and Cathy wondered whether it wasn't just a marketing ploy by the water boards and the soft beverage industry. After all, if you gave up the booze, you had to have something to replace it.

What, then, happened in February, when throats were supposedly as dry as a penguin's tongue, seeking cheer and comfort from a favourite tipple? Lent! Lent happened in February, relentlessly unforgiving, coming swiftly on the heels of a dry, abstemious January and requiring – from the Christian community at least – a steadfastness of spirit that prolonged their self-imposed purgatory for the forty days to Easter. It was a tough cookie indeed, thought Cathy, that could survive Dry January to then almost immediately have to face the rigours of Lent that not only lasted longer but had a weighty commitment to God attached. She hoped He appreciated it.

Pancake Day, that annual herald of the discipline to come, trumpeted a last supper of flour, eggs and milk. Cathy had often confused the ingredients with those for making glue, with disastrous results at a supper for friends, one of whom had taken revenge by adding pink colouring to her mixture for the next batch, making her pancakes look like limp bits of flesh. She had not repeated the evening.

Cathy had previously always enjoyed pancakes – the sweet type, not the savoury variety that people went in for these days, filled with tomatoes and cheese or chorizo, bacon and chilli. Why chefs had to muck about with the traditional recipe was anyone's guess, but it was not for her. Give her lemon and sugar any time and she was happy – before the supper evening, of course.

Pancake Day was a moveable feast, dependent on the Easter festival, itself determined by the first full moon on or after the twenty-first of March, an approximation of the spring equinox set by the Christian Church and linked to the Jewish feast of Passover. It was also called Shrove Tuesday or *Mardi Gras* – Fat Tuesday  which sat rather badly with

Cathy, the spare tyre round her waist being testament to the many rich foods consumed ahead of the Lenten fast. Not just on Tuesday either but on the preceding Saturday, Sunday and Monday, if not earlier still.

Once a year Lent came around and was in many ways like New Year, its resolutions faithfully made only to be broken on day two. She always started out with such good intentions. It was only forty days if you didn't include Sundays and the weeks seemed to fly by the older she became. How difficult could it be? As a child, she'd given up chocolate, or biscuits, or sweets, when she'd really wanted to say no to vegetables or trips to the dentist when her fillings fell out; but her mum was made of sterner stuff and set the rules in Cathy's house, so she struggled on through the dark days of Lent, wishing she could abandon her faith and leave deprivation behind.

As an adult, she pondered what to give up, her old religion still drawing her in, however hard she tried to resist. Food, of course, was the obvious choice – cakes and cream teas, meals out with friends – but the shops were full of hot cross buns and why make life worse in the cold winter months? Instead, Cathy thought, she could do something worthy, like cooking for the elderly or donating blood but Cathy was squeamish and remembered her pancakes and ruled out both before Lent had begun.

The older she grew, the harder she found it to comply with the pressures and mores of the day. If the spirit was willing, the flesh was weak, 'though the spirit quite frequently failed her too. Even the dentist was hard on her now, commenting on the state of her teeth: the enamel was being worn away (eat less fruit!) and her teeth were looking very stained (drink less tea!). Goodness, there'd be no pleasures left soon if the doctors and health gurus had their way. Cathy knew what the answer was and laughed as she looked them all in the face – to give up on giving up and have done with them all.

# THE DO IT YOURSELF! CUSTOMER

It had all started at the petrol pump. Mark remembered well, his older brother Steve champing at the bit when trying to impress his girl in his new Ford Capri with the forecourt attendant refusing to budge. The system had changed, with little publicity (or none that he'd heard) and he was forced to lift the nozzle himself, his girlfriend giggling at his frenzied state as petrol dripped on his winkle picker shoes. Not only had it spoiled his big night out but he wasn't even offered a discount while made to do all the work himself. Matters weren't helped by his girlfriend's suggestion that they buy a tandem and save all the trouble. Her laughter ringing in his ears, he ended the relationship there and then. He'd look for a girl who understood.

Next came the strawberry fields. *Pick your own!* the posters cheerfully cried, their bold and colourful lettering luring you into a muddy field after the usual rains of a typical English summer. Mark and his family had sometimes gone, the promise of cheaper fruit being the ultimate draw, though it never seemed to turn out that way.

The family dispersed in different directions, its members aiming to outdo each other in finding the biggest and juiciest nuggets. Others, of course, had been there first, not least the farmer who'd gathered the best, boxing them up to sell at market.

Never defeated, the family moved on, with breaking backs and aching knees, picking their strawberries one at a time and eating several in the process, determined to get their money's worth. On meeting up in the queue to pay, Mark examined the family spoils, aghast at the bagloads each member had. Putting them on the scales to be weighed, Mark stared in disbelief. Twenty-eight pounds of delicious red berries, far less sweet when he came to pay, his wallet now as broken as his back. Thank God they didn't weigh his kids with their red stained T-shirts over bellies round and full.

Mark understood how his brother once felt, staring down the barrel of development years ago at the petrol pumps. It was the thin end of the wedge of course, as the years rolled by and progress marched on, flattening the weak and unsuspecting in its wake.

His wife, indeed, was another victim, having lost her "job for life" at the bank. Nobody came to the teller anymore, preferring instead to queue outside, waiting to talk to a cold, hard machine which, if having a bad day, would chew up your debit card in a flash. Many banks had already closed, their business having moved online with more and more people forced to do the same. Like it or not, it was the way of the world, those without computers or newfangled devices being dragged along behind and in search of help elsewhere. The industrial revolution all over again, with those in favour and those against. Mark, his wife and his brother Steve were firmly in the latter camp.

You could even order your shopping online if you didn't want to wait in the shop, though Mark and his wife still went in person, not trusting their food to be still in date if left to the whims of the packers in store.

The shopping experience was not as it was, and you struggled to find an assistant to help. Most of the desks were now self-service, a cashier only evident after ten o'clock when a mighty queue would start to form of those with trolleys and the weekly shop.

Shopping had never been Mark's bag but complaining was, when justified. How was a trolleyload of food meant to fit in the bagging area that had been designed for baskets alone? You couldn't scan and pack on your own and half the items weren't recognised by the machine supposedly meant to help. The bagging area rejected your bag, and some of the goods were without a bar code, forcing you then to flag down a helper to run and seek the relevant aisle in the forlorn hope of finding some labelled. Just as you hoped to be nearing the end, you found you were meant to have weighed loose goods that ended up being left behind, heaped sadly upon a graveyard of veg, forsaken by shoppers mourning their loss. It was all a veritable nightmare.

You'd never have to leave your home if the powers that be had their way and never have to speak to a soul except by way of an automated voice that repeatedly said you were twelfth in the queue before cutting you off half an hour in. This was the case with the doctor's surgery where you were lucky now to reach the receptionist, let alone have the chance to speak to a medic unless you'd completed your online form.

Mark knew where all this was headed: DIY surgery before too long. A diagram with dotted lines, "cut here" written along the body. He only hoped the instructions were clear and you had a sharp enough knife to do it, unless you could order a scalpel online, gauze and sutures included in the box.

The final curtain only remained, your coffin a flat pack to assemble yourself. "Three other people are looking online, order now as they're selling out fast." Climb inside and press a button and off you go on motorised wheels, your self-service funeral ready and waiting, sealed and delivered from your very own home.

# JUNIOR

He's called Junior, my crow. Junior. That's his name. That's the name I gave him when he first arrived. He may have another, but I don't know what it is as I don't speak crow. He may have tried to tell me – several times, possibly – but I call him Junior and he doesn't seem to mind.

I'm not sure who his mum is, or his dad, or whether he has siblings. He might in any case be an orphan now. He's one of my family, is Junior. Always has been. He knows it and so do I.

He's coming up for three now, Junior, and not much has changed since he first arrived. I remember seeing him for the first time, standing on the lawn, quite distinct from his fellow crows. Not white or anything peculiar, just the usual glossy black, but he had a couple of tints of grey on him like he'd been to the barber for some dye. I thought they must be baby bird markings, but Junior still has them three years on, and they help to distinguish him when seen out of context away from the back garden.

Junior is a carrion crow, though his markings are more commonly found on the neck of the family's smaller member, the jackdaw, the only black bird with a grey nape. His thigh feathers lie tight to his body, giving him a smoother appearance than that of his cousin the rook with his ruffled and baggy trousers, making Junior the cool dude of the corvids.

The large black raven, typically seen in open and hilly country or in rocky and woody habitats, is Junior's most famous relative, regally residing at the Tower of London, a celebrity amongst crows though with his wings clipped to stop him from flying away. Since the reign of Charles II, ravens have always been kept at the Tower, the legend advising that without them, both Crown and Tower would fall. Guardians then, of King and Keep, the ravens are special birds indeed but Junior, for me, is the best bird of all.

Intelligent and adaptable (like most birds but particularly the corvids), Junior has a character all of his own. He knows my garden is his food emporium and knows if he calls, I will come. He doesn't even have to call these days, his adorable little head tilt sending me rushing for food. Junior is a ground feeder, a scavenger mostly, taking whatever's there already and certainly anything I tend to put out, his favourite food being bread and suet balls. He has competition for both, the magpie and the fox being fond of a fat ball and the pigeons with their sights on the bread. They don't stop Junior from having his fill and although he's a little ungainly on his pins, he's regularly seen making off with the suet, the entire ball in his mouth like an over-large pimple on his big black beak.

He always comes on his own, does Junior, proving the old country saying that "a rook on its own is a crow, a crow in a crowd is a rook". Not unsociable, crows often gather for warmth, safety and family conferences and you must wonder what they might be plotting when they come together in very large numbers. A collection of crows is called a murder, a group of ravens a conspiracy, leading some to link them with death and darkness, though their black mourning dress doesn't help them with that. They are also known to care for their dead, gathering round as if at a funeral, but this may have more to do with danger and a state of alert while they watch for predators.

Their connection with death may be well known, playing with the minds of the superstitious, but there is an alternative view of the corvid family, coming from spiritual association and giving a far more positive slant.

In the Bible, after the great flood, it is the raven that Noah first sends forth (ahead of the dove and other creatures), trusting it to check if the land is dry. Elsewhere in the Bible, the raven brings sustenance to those in need and, in his turn, is cared for and provided for by God.

For Native Americans, the crow was considered a messenger of good fortune, of opportunity and transformation, while for the Ancient Greeks, the crow brought messages from the gods. It features too in many mythologies, from Norse to Celtic and early English legend – in which it is said that King Arthur did not die but was turned into a raven or Cornish chough. In the West Country and Wales, the raven was considered a royal bird, for this very reason it might be assumed.

Junior, then, has important ancestry and we can look at him now with a new perspective and admiration. Perhaps he's aware, when strutting his stuff, of his long and interesting lineage. It behoves us all to take great heed – it might be King Arthur we're looking at. Long live my Junior! Long live the King!

# A GUINEA PIG UNDER THE SHED

"Do you think it's dead?"

"Oh crikey, don't say that."

"It's not moving. It hasn't moved for ages."

"See if you can give it a poke with that stick."

"I can't reach it. It's too far under."

"What are we going to do? We can't just leave it."

"Let's wait ten minutes. Leave it alone and come back."

"We should never have agreed to take this on. We don't know the first thing about pets."

"It's only a guinea pig."

"Yes, but why let it out in the garden?"

"I thought it would like a little run. Get some fresh air or something. It's been cooped up in the house all week."

"Yes, well it's had a little run. It's stuck under the shed now."

"Come on, let's go in."

"We can't just leave it. It might run away."

"Run away where?!"

"Well, *I* don't know, but we can't leave it here. We've got to do *something*. Try calling it."

"Calling it?! Are you mad?"

"Try calling it!!"

"What's its name?"

"Tilly. Tilly Pig."

"Bloody hell."

"Call it!!"

"Tilly! Tilly, Tilly, Tilly, Tilly, Tilly."

"It's no use. He's not listening."

"How the hell can you tell that?!"

"His ears aren't moving."

"What?! Nothing's moving! He's dead I tell you."

"Well, we can't leave him here or the fox will eat him."

"Lucky fox! They're a delicacy in Peru."

"Oh, do take this seriously. We've got to *do* something."

"Like what?"

"Talk to him."

"*You* talk to him!"

"I don't speak Spanish."

"Neither do I! Hasn't he learnt English yet?"

"Oh, for pity's sake, *do* something. PLEASE!"

"Perhaps we could frighten him out."

"How?"

"I don't know. Pretend you're a fox. Bark or something."

"Don't be silly. The neighbours will hear me and think I'm mad."

"I know who *will* be mad when they come home from holiday. Steve and Sue."

"Tilly! Tilly!"

"Come on Tilly. Stop messing about."

"Get him some food. A few of those biscuits. He likes those."

"Aren't they the cat's?"

"She won't mind. We'll get her some more."

"Could we buy another guinea pig? Bury this one and buy another."

"Oh, stop it! PLEASE! Can't you revive it?"

"How??"

"*I* don't know."

"Kiss of life?!"

"Tut. You sure it's dead?"

"Yes, I think so. It hasn't moved for ages now."

"It's so dark under there. Poor little thing. Narrow too. How did it get there in the first place? There's barely enough room to squeeze under."

"I don't really know. Didn't you see it?"

"No, I was still inside. I thought *you'd* seen it."

"No, I didn't. I just followed you."

"Sshh. What was that?"

"What?"

"I heard a squeak."

"A squeak from where?"

"Look behind you! It's Tilly! *Tilly!*"

"Then who is that under the shed??"

# KATHLEEN CONTEMPLATES

Kathleen was up early. 6 a.m. As usual. All old people are up early, she thought. Why is that? Do they need less sleep or are they now just restless after a life of worry, toil, experience and heartache? Good times too, of course, but it's the worries that keep you awake, that and wondering what comes next.

Did she turn the gas off before going to bed? Did she lock the doors? Did she check or did it even matter these days? Of course it mattered, Kathleen snorted to herself, jolting herself back to positivity, annoyed she'd thought otherwise. She had never been a negative person, all her life struggling to understand those who were and really having little time for them. She didn't suffer fools gladly, she chuckled.

Life was different now though. Harder somehow. Sometimes the mind, always the body. It was just as well that bus pass wasn't allowed until 9.30 as it took so long to get ready these days. All those years ago, skipping happily along the street as a little girl, she never thought she'd end up like this, creaking and wobbly. Goodness, it was an effort to get out of bed most days, especially when dark and the heating hadn't yet kicked in.

She always kept a dressing gown on top of the bed, that nice flannel one her friend had brought back from her holiday in Scarborough. A strange present she'd thought at the time – people normally brought back shell animals or some local craft or other – but it had certainly seen some use this winter and she was glad of its warmth and comfort.

Using her bedside chair to steady herself, Kathleen stood for a moment, in her dressing gown and slippers, before moving off slowly towards the bathroom and then on downstairs, one step at a time, holding the rail on both sides while imagining herself downhill skiing, goggles on her head and slicing through the snow. *Bend zee knees!* If only she could!

Ooh, how she looked forward to her morning cup of tea. The first one of the day was always the best, a good Yorkshire brew, nice and strong. You wouldn't get that at the *après-ski*, that's for sure. More like a spritz or a bombardino.

Kathleen had been skiing once and thoroughly enjoyed it, cutting a dash in her ice-blue snow pants, attracting all the young men with her tall, sylph-like figure, carved turns and general derring-do. A long time ago now, for Kathleen had shrunk with the years and through recent ill health. Cancer had ravished her, thinned out her hair and left her a sorrowful shadow of her former upright self. Physically poor, her determination by contrast remained strong and she continued to dye her hair well into her eighties, bright colours to match her personality and outlook on life. Age and illness had diminished neither her spark nor her childhood wish to rule the world. Feisty still, she always won a debate and awoke each day ready to straighten out life's global problems. She could teach that government a thing or two, outwitting and outclassing them in knowledge, vision and skill and even showing them how to dress. Smart and chic was Kathleen with an Italian style derived from her years in Milan.

That was her task for today. A shopping expedition, to find a new outfit for young Saoirse's wedding. Something timeless that complimented her looks, her still-warm smile and those blue eyes that sparkled. Spring chicken she was not, but what was wrong with an ageing hen in the winter of one's life? Yes, Kathleen decided, she could stride out with the best of them still. One foot forward and then the other, in three-inch heels and patent leather, *Louboutin* if she could get them.

Kathleen smiled as she knew she'd outshine them, the wedding group in their modern clothes. Even the bride, in her off-white creation, was never a match for a daughter of Milan. Kathleen mused at the thought of her kitten heels as she glanced down at her furry slippers, cosy and warm on her bunioned feet. Feet that would take her upstairs again now, to prepare herself for the day ahead. Into the bathroom to wash all down, taking her time as she always did, easing the flannel over her body, nice hot water on dried-out skin. Then for the teeth, as the dentist ordered, upper and lower, back and front. It all took time and all took effort but couldn't be left and had to be done, however hard the task these days.

Bending over the sink was less of an option than it had been before, but trying to stand upright for any length of time was not an easy task either. Kathleen worried that the day might come when she could no longer clean her teeth at all. Appearance had always mattered to her, but she was still able to laugh at the sight in the mirror of a mouthful of potholes where teeth had once been. That was the character she was. Standing there now, with her Oral B, she weaved her brush in and out, like making lace on a dental doily. Gentle and slow to avoid more damage but ready now for a long sit-down. The shopping spree would have to wait.

# GOOSEBERRY FOOL

She wished she hadn't invited him now. Her younger brother James was always welcome, of course, and she loved his conversation and witty repartee, but she knew now that she'd chosen the wrong night. She didn't know that last week when she saw him at the dance, but so much had happened since then and she knew she couldn't retract her offer. Not now when his wife had dumped him after twenty years of marriage. She'd only seen them at the ball last week and thought how happy they looked as they glided over the floor together. How life had changed in just a few short days. So unexpected. So unfair. Life could be cruel sometimes.

For Shirley, however, the opposite had happened. Well, almost. Having found herself single for the last umpteen years – her own significant half having left her for someone younger (and less attractive, Shirley thought) – she'd finally met a man. Yes! Her! Shirley! After all this time, having reconciled herself to being on her own forever! Shirley Roberts, 51, not unfriendly, not unintelligent, and keeping her figure and pretty face. Someone at last had spotted her and what a catch he was!

Out of nowhere he crossed the floor – Richard Simmonds, six feet tall, dark and handsome and heading her way. She thought at first he'd seen someone else, someone he knew, someone to flirt with, but all of a sudden, he stood in front of her, brushing the hair from his suntanned face and smiling from ear to ear. His eyes were deep and dark as the night and Shirley felt herself melting into them as his low, soft voice asked her to dance.

Boy, what a dancer he was! He knew all the steps, surprising for a man, though it later transpired he'd been taking lessons once a week at the assembly rooms. They'd certainly paid off, Shirley thought, and she was only left wondering if she should take some herself, as she felt out of practice beside this man. It didn't, however, seem to matter as he guided her about the room effortlessly and full of smiles. So many people stopped to look at this beautiful couple who stole the floor with their foxtrot, waltz and cha cha cha.

At the end of a joyous and magical night, he walked her home, asking to see her the following day. Shirley accepted readily and the two then met every night.

Richard worked at the local hospital as a heart consultant (or cardiologist). Shirley could have guessed that much as this kind, caring and adorable guy knew all about hearts and how they beat. What a wonderful job to have, helping those who needed to heal, restoring their life and happiness. She couldn't have found a better man.

And so it was that she'd invited him to dinner, on the very day she'd asked her brother. How could she let either down, her handsome, new, gorgeous love or her sad and lonely brother James? She knew the two would get on well but, goodness me, that wasn't the point. She wanted Richard to herself but couldn't risk upsetting James. How had she come to mix up the days and ask the two to come together?! There was nothing for it but to go ahead.

The evening came, a Friday night, and Shirley was busy in the kitchen. She'd gone to a lot of trouble that day, scouring through her recipe books, then sourcing the food at the local shops. She so wanted to impress this man while James, she knew, would devour anything. He'd offered, however, to make a dessert, with the gooseberries from his summer garden and Shirley was pleased to accept his help.

The first course was a smoked salmon pâté, easy to eat and light on the tongue and sure to please her medical man. She hadn't used her blender for a while but remembered not to touch the blade, as she didn't want blood all over the fish! A doctor he may be but Richard must see enough of that not to want it again for his dinner!

She tasted the mousse as she went along, to check the amount of lemon and salt. She couldn't resist the double cream, white and smooth on the end of her spoon, thick and rich and full of flavour.

She decided to make an art of the meal, by wrapping the mousse in extra salmon, folding it in like a little parcel.

How lovely her new ramekins looked with the pink smoked salmon nestling within, a light sprig of dill resting on top. These would be chilled until ready to eat, when she'd serve them with pieces of melba toast, dry and crisp and perfect for pâté. A nice Sancerre to accompany the meal with its pungent aroma of gooseberries.

For the main, she had chosen a chicken dish with chestnut mushrooms and truffle oil, to keep the meat as moist as she could and give it a distinct earthy flavour. Shirley followed a recipe, carefully studying every line, keen to create a special meal that would keep her man coming back and win him over, heart and soul.

Into the pan went onions and garlic, finely chopped and cooked till soft in melted butter on a moderate heat. After that came the chestnut mushrooms, gently fried till their moisture reduced. Shirley drizzled in the truffle oil, added some decadent truffle paste, some flat-leaf parsley and ground black pepper. She stirred it all to a nice, smooth texture, enjoying the woody and musky smell that floated around on a hidden wave.

Placing the chicken at the side of the pan, she spread the mixture beneath its skin as evenly as she possibly could before patting the chicken into shape and basting it with a little butter. She popped it into its roasting tin, covering with a sheet of foil and carefully placing in the oven, to roast away until nicely browned. Later on, she would make a salad and cook some rice, like a nice risotto with its creamy, comforting and pleasing taste.

All she needed now was James to turn up with his gooseberry fool ahead of her main evening guest, the delightful and ever-so-handsome Richard. True to his word, James arrived, but an hour before she expected him to. As she opened the door, there he stood, carrying two, very tall glasses full of fruit, yoghurt and cream.

"Gooseberry fool!" her brother cried as if he was heralding April the first. "Did you really think I would spoil your night and sit playing gooseberry to you and your beau? Take these quickly before Richard arrives and have a truly lovely time." With that, he was off into the night, leaving Shirley with tears in her eyes. Not only had she a nice new man, but she also had a lovely brother who was going home to beans on toast while she and Richard ate gooseberry fool.

# ESTELLE AND EZEKIEL

I was attracted to Estelle from our first encounter. Like a star in the night sky, she simply dazzled. She lit up a room as she floated in, an ageless sprite with an ethereal beauty. She said I attracted her too, drew her to me like a magnet, turning her head with my heavenly body and transcendental being.

We fell for each other, literally and metaphorically, spiralling down from a giddy height, gaining speed till we hit the ground and the earth became our reality. Clinging together with no way back, we formed a home, a quiet space away from the crowd, hidden away so no one could hurt us. When the light had gone and all was dark, we loved to stand in the garden and gaze, tracing our path on the celestial map and dreaming of the life beyond.

We were in the garden that night, the night the object first appeared, moving across the sky like Zeus' chariot. Out of this world for ordinary folk, our neighbours did not understand it, the government did not understand it, wise men did not understand it. They tried to shoot it from the sky through fear and lack of understanding.

Back it came, night after night, crossing the skies, searching, searching, crossing continents, never landing. In between the stars it went, round the planets, past the moon, leaving in its wake a mystery: where did it come from and for whom?

On the earth, men were shouting, firing missiles into the sky, but nothing could touch the speeding object circling above and far too high.

As winter drew on, the crisis deepened across the globe. Talks were held in every country, in every town and foreign tongue. Then nothing for nights, the object vanished, disappearing as quickly as it had come. Until one night, a fireball, an explosion of light rent the sky in two. The object returned in a blaze of glory, now come to claim its due.

We stepped from the house into our garden, watching the skies from whence it came. Estelle was transformed at that very moment, bursting into resplendent light as the wheels of the chariot turned towards us. Hand outstretched to take me with her, we lifted up from our tellurian state. A final flash, then total silence, a mantle of darkness covered the earth, and we were gone from sight.

Home, Ezekiel, home from exile.

# THE LETTER

Lizzie was not looking forward to this job. There were many tasks she hated, like dusting, ironing and cleaning the oven but they were what she called "necessary jobs" even though she did them as infrequently as she could possibly manage. Clearing the loft was another matter but it had to be tackled before her move up north in a couple of months.

Some of her friends put nothing in their lofts, believing that if it was up there it wasn't needed and therefore shouldn't be stashed away in the first place. There was a lot to be said for this but then where would she have put those large cardboard boxes that might come in handy one day or the Christmas decorations that only came out once a year and which would otherwise be cluttering up a cupboard. The trouble was, as the years went by, more and more items had been added to the loft and now, after nearly thirty years in her Hampshire home, she could barely walk from one side to the other. A daunting task lay ahead of Lizzie and one which she could unfortunately no longer put off. It simply had to be done.

She knew that she would find no treasures, as it was only she who had put stuff up there and, although she couldn't recall exactly what she had hidden away, she was very certain there was nothing of value. Goodness knows, she had little of value anyway and if she had, it would be on display, not tucked away where no one could see it. She frequently marvelled at the *Antiques Roadshow* where every other person seemed to find a priceless object, either in the loft, forgotten or unknown about, or while rummaging in charity shops or church bazaars. Lizzie had nothing like that, only tat and broken toys, mildewed magazines and useless empty boxes. Hopefully much could be just thrown away without the need to sift through it all, wasting more precious time, time she no longer had. She pondered once if she dared just leave it but that would be dreadful for the new owners to find, and she couldn't bring herself to do it. Lizzie was a kind woman who always put others first. Leaving her rubbish would be a despicable act and she'd never forgive herself for it.

She set aside the whole of the weekend for the mountain she had to climb. Kitted out in overalls and clear plastic gloves, her hair tied back in an Alice band, Lizzie mounted the ladder to the loft, carrying a large bottle of water and a packet of chocolate digestives to keep her going as she sifted through the rubble.

Sitting down with a heavy sigh, Lizzie began her indomitable task. Hour after hour she went through the clutter, making – it seemed – precious little headway, the jumble before her never looking to diminish and almost seeming to grow further still. Frustrated and dirty, Lizzie paused to look at the scene, wondering how she would ever clear it and promising never to repeat the ordeal. There was something to be said for minimalism, although Lizzie knew she was one of life's hoarders and that anything leaving the house was always a wrench.

As darkness fell and she thought about tea, Lizzie's eyes lit upon a small scrap of paper poking up between the packing cases she'd used to floor the loft, barely noticeable amongst all the debris and other lumber. Stretching across on her hands and knees, she lifted the paper from its moorings and gently unfolded it as it started to crumble between her fingers.

Lizzie stared, open-mouthed, at the beautiful manuscript there before her. Hard to read, this elegant hand, but her eye began to trace each letter, gradually allowing her to understand its content. Nobody wrote like this anymore. It was all Times Roman or Arial with nothing of the individuality seen herein.

Frightened to move lest the paper disintegrate, Lizzie peered at the words before her, written in ink with a fine quill pen, scratchy in places with a few crossings-out. Lizzie smiled at the witty text, its author showing a fine sense of humour, subtle in places, acerbic in others. A talented hand, written with ease and comfortable with the intended reader, trusting and honest in its sentiment.

The letter itself told of a lover, a *beau* as he would then have been called, one who'd captured the heart of the author who found herself inclining to love. Balls were described with flirtatious dancing, the handsome young pair in a world of their own. Standing up together so often, less prudent than the time allowed, the excitement it caused could only be guessed at, comments made behind fluttering fans.

As Lizzie read on through the letter, she became aware to whom the words were addressed. The name Cassandra struck a chord and she suddenly realised, as she glanced at the date, that this was a letter from her heroine Jane Austen, written to her sister in 1796. Shaking now and filled with wonder, Lizzie marvelled at the thought, that this was a letter lost in time, thought to have been destroyed by the faithful Cassandra, fearful for her sister's good reputation being unwittingly ruined by a fleeting fancy for an Irish charmer who inspired love before departing for home. Lizzie stared at the letter and smiled. She had something of value after all.

# WHEN THE FUTURE COMES EARLY

It seemed a long time ago now, but it was only three years. She remembered that holiday well and with great fondness. They'd driven to St Ives together from their cottage in Penzance. A week never seemed enough when they came down to Cornwall as there was always so much to fit in, always so much to see.

They'd stopped off in Fowey for a night, as Hazel was keen to visit Menabilly, the one-time home of Daphne Du Maurier and inspiration for her fictional Manderley. They'd then travelled on via Truro and Helston before finally reaching Penzance itself, where a paddle in the sea was considered essential, if somewhat cold at that time of year.

Both women just loved Cornwall and it was always a joy to them to return, to visit old haunts and discover places new. They'd been coming together for a good few years now and St Ives was always on the list. First stop, the Hepworth Museum, to sit in the garden and admire the sculptures, smooth and sensuous, round and beautiful, works of art that you wanted to touch, to let your hand glide over their forms and sense the skill that had moulded them.

On through the town to the beach and an ice cream, fending off gulls and others in the queue, to savour the last of a honeycomb scoop before taking a walk along the front and then on up to the Chapel of St Nicholas overlooking the Atlantic waves. They were lucky to see the seals again, round heads bobbing up through the water, then ducking down to emerge out at sea. Hazel and Tina could sit for hours watching these amazing creatures, but all too soon they had to go back, return to the Square where the bus awaited to carry them up the hill to the car park.

The two friends were the first to board and settled down for the ride uphill. A steep climb if done on foot, they always chose the bus these days – less wear and tear, as Hazel would say. They watched as others took their seats, trying to resist the urge to stare, for each knew what the other was thinking – that their fellow passengers all looked the same, like part of a secret cult. Elderly women with short, permed hair, scarves round their necks and warm winter coats, buttoned up tightly in the cool spring air. Their gentlemen folk followed along, cracking little jokes and carrying the bags. A coach party surely or package tour.

It was then that Tina had her vision, of an ugly future as it seemed to her then. She saw herself and her best friend Hazel, walking with sticks and needing help, no longer enjoying their independent travel but part of a group, a herd of sheep, in a line, one behind the other. She saw them dressed in warmer clothes, in woolly layers and thicker vests, content to follow another's lead instead of working it out for themselves. Altogether a different breed, like the sheep they were destined to become.

Hazel had laughed and told her off and said they would never lose their spark. They'd still eat ices and swim in the sea, even in the colder months. They'd still go looking for shells together, still find pleasure in quirkiness, dance barefooted on long wet grass and howl at the moon come the winter solstice. Nothing would change between the friends, and nothing would ever come between them.

It was a shock to them both when Tina had her stroke, less than a year after their trip to Cornwall. Tina, of all people. One of the fittest, healthiest people around – until then. It struck her down like lightning felling a tree and, as yet, she remained afflicted, paralysed on her right-hand side, forcing her to rely on others, something she'd always hoped not to do.

Hazel had bought her a motorised chair from a win she'd had on the premium bonds. She insisted on spending it all on her friend and helping her as much as she could. She knew, had it been the other way round, that Tina would have done the same for her, the two friends having always been close. Tina could walk with a stick, just about, but her gait was ungainly and always off balance. She hated now to go out on her own, ever worried she'd take a fall or topple over in her Ferrari chair. She knew it didn't go that fast but feared the kerbs and broken pavements. Caterpillar wheels would do the trick but might look odd in Surbiton.

When Hazel came at the end of the day, as she always did after work, Tina suggested a little break. Perhaps the two could return to Cornwall, visit some old familiar places, watch the seals at Godrevy Point, admire the surfers at Sennen Cove.

Two weeks later, by overnight sleeper, they arrived in Penzance with the rest of the group. A package tour had had to be booked, as Hazel had still not learnt to drive. The two old friends boarded the coach and looked at each other knowingly. Neither had had to plan the trip, the itinerary already organised. Nor were the meals in *ad hoc* places, but all at set times within the hotel. Their fellow travellers were of an age and looked at the girls pityingly. The holiday wasn't the same at all, though alright they supposed. There and then they made a vow – Hazel would learn to drive on return and Tina would source the best ice cream. Next time they came, they'd just come together, party till dawn, eat pasties on the beach. While they had each other and a life to lead, Tina's vision would have to wait.

# COUCH TO 5K

Johnnie Weston had never been into sport. He didn't mind watching it on the telly, a bit of darts or sometimes the snooker, but even that bored him after a while. He was not what you'd call an active man, much to the annoyance of his wife Belinda, who'd always wished for some get-up-and-go, however far he got up and went. Ten years of marriage had crushed that dream and she accepted the reality lying ahead. If she wanted a holiday, she'd go with her friend, an old school chum who lived on her own, always ready for fun and adventure and willing to go at the drop of a hat. Catherine would go to the opening of an envelope, money to hand and bag ready packed, needing no persuasion to head for the door, yearning for excitement and places new. So many paths they had travelled together, enriching their lives and enjoying themselves, while Johnnie sat still on his comfy couch, both feet up and reading the paper, stirring only to make the next cup of tea. Why would he want to travel at all when all that he needed was here at home? Leave the trips to the girls, he thought, as he stretched for a biscuit to dunk in his tea.

It astonished them all when he one day announced he was taking up running at the end of the week. At school he'd always been known as Slug, so slow was he to move at all and only then to look for food. His friends had laughed at his lumbering physique and Slug had laughed with them, not caring at all. Escaping the regular cross-country runs, by hiding away or pretending to be ill, Slug lay low till the coast was clear, emerging only when ready to do so, usually when fancying a tasty snack. He'd rarely in life thought about diet, scoffing at every passing fad, while slowly piling on the pounds as others slimmed and honed their bodies. Each to his own, he always thought.

When Dave called round to see his friend, he found him lying on the couch, covered in crumbs and half asleep. Dave and Slug were kindred spirits, enjoying their pint and packet of crisps every Sunday at the Dog and Duck. The pub was the only one in the village and barely yards from either one's house, so neither had more than a few steps to walk and no effort was ever involved. Dave had come now on an urgent mission and needed his friend to help him out. The doctor's house, a few doors down, had just been sold to somebody new. A beautiful woman, their new GP, single and arriving in a matter of weeks. Dave was keen to woo this stunner but needed now to slim down fast. He and his friend could take up running, or jogging as he thought it was called. Either way, they could take it up, as many a man had done before them, not always in hot pursuit of a woman

Dave had heard of *Couch to 5k*, a popular craze at the start of the year when tummies were full of Christmas tuck and summer holidays were round the corner. Everyone wanted a beach-ready body, everyone save Johnnie and Dave. This though, was May, and it mattered not, as the end result would be the same and Dave could stand before his new doctor, lithe and lovely and ready to please. He needed his friend to help him out by running with him and urging him on.

Succumbing reluctantly to the cause, Slug felt bound to acquiesce, putting down the biscuit tin and savouring his very last bite. They'd start on Friday and work from there with a well-planned route to avoid prying eyes and curtains twitching in the village.

Friday came and the friends set forth, walking first at a leisurely pace, then breaking slowly into a trot like a newly cut gelding finding its way. The discomfort they felt was not dissimilar as legs began to rub together and denim jeans began to chafe. Neither was properly kitted out and that in time would have to change if the two were ever to look the part.

Three times a week they were meant to run, with a day of rest in between. Inexperienced and out of breath, every step taking its toll, the two friends stopped and started, red in the face and unable to speak. Perhaps they were taking it far too fast or needed to find a better rhythm, as the end of each run saw the pair with very stiff legs and feet full of blisters. At least the two were sleeping at night, out for the count as their heads hit the pillow.

Week Two came and went, with the friends now clothed in tracksuits and trainers, cutting a dash in looks at least and gradually starting to enjoy themselves. Why had they not done this before, they asked each other as they picked up speed. The early morning air was welcome, as indeed were the cheers as they ran through the village, no longer having to hide their shame at having once been so unfit. Already progress had been made, their energy levels now increasing with every new corner turned and every new path taken.

Finally reaching the end of Week Nine, Johnnie and Dave slapped themselves on the back, wondrous at their great achievement, startled at their new-found pleasure. Both had come a very long way, in distance yes, but goals met too. Slug had shed his very being, a transformation so complete, a butterfly leaving behind the chrysalis, an ugly duckling now a swan. Dave strode out in new, light chinos, shirt tucked in revealing his shape, round no more but tall and slender, ready to woo his lady friend.

Gone were the crisps and pints of beer, gone were the couch and biscuit tin, as 5k stretched to ten with wedding bells caught on a distant breeze.

# THE ART CLASS

CHARACTERS:
> The mother, Pat
> The father, Gerry
> The son, Joe

SCENE:
The small hallway of an ordinary suburban house in northwest London. Coats are hanging on pegs just inside the door to the right. Beneath them, a jumble of boots and shoes have been left haphazardly on an old mat. Opposite the front door, stairs lead up to the bedrooms and bathroom. Leading off the downstairs hallway, almost immediately to the left, the living room, giving on to the street and, at the other end, the garden. Through the hallway and past the stairs, lies the kitchen, at the entrance to which most of the dialogue takes place.

The mother is in her early fifties, of average height and slim build, a pretty woman with long, light brown hair, held at the back by a large ornate clip. Standing at the foot of the stairs, left hand on the banister, she calls up to her son.

Pat – Joe, have you got a minute? (*She moves to the door of the kitchen.*)

Joe – Yep, be right there. (*Joe comes down, running his hand through his curly hair and looking half asleep.*)

Pat – (*looking serious*) Hi, Joe. Erm, this is a bit delicate.

Joe – (*looking puzzled*) What's the matter?

Pat – I found these in your room earlier. (*She hands him a pile of photos – around a dozen of them.*)

Joe – (*angrily*) Why were you in my room?

Pat – I was just gathering the washing you said you wanted doing.

Joe – (*shuffling on the spot, looking somewhat embarrassed*) Well, what about them?

Pat – They're photos of naked men. Virile naked men. All of them.

Joe – So?

Pat – (*exasperated*) So?? What are you doing with them? (*Joe doesn't reply. Silence for a moment.*)

Pat – Where did you get them, Joe?

Joe – They're for my art class. We're doing life drawing.

Pat – (*incredulous and shaking her head*) No. Don't give me that. This isn't life drawing. They're pornographic!!!

Joe – (*raising his voice a little*) No, Mum! They're for my class.

Pat – What sort of a class is that?!

Joe – I told you. We're doing life drawing.

Pat – But these aren't drawings, they're photos! Pretty vivid ones too!!

(*Joe turns away and starts to move off.*)

Pat – (*loudly*) Come back here!

Joe – I'm going to my room.

Pat – (*more insistent*) No. You're staying here. I want an explanation. A proper one.

Joe – I told you what they're for.

Pat – And I don't believe you. Whose are they? Who took them?

Joe – I don't know.

Pat – You must know who gave them to you.

Joe – (*shifting on the spot*) I'm not saying.

Pat – This is serious, Joe. Tell me, please, where did you get them?

(*Joe remains silent.*)

Pat – Who gave them to you?

(*Joe still remains silent.*)

Pat. – What were you going to do with them?

Joe – (*sighing*) I've told you already.

Pat – Don't lie to me, Joe. I know you're lying.

Joe – I'm going to my room.

Pat – Give me back those photos. (*She pauses.*) I'm getting your dad.

Joe – No! Please, Mum! Don't get Dad!

Pat – Then tell me the truth.

(*Joe is silent. Pat walks away. She can be heard opening the back door and calling her husband, Gerry, who is in the garden. Pat and Joe then remain in silence, Pat looking at Joe, Joe looking at the floor, until Gerry comes in.*)

Gerry – What's up?

Pat – Give them to your father, Joe.

(*Joe hands him the pile of photos.*)

Pat – I found those in his room. He says they're for his art class. Art class!!

(*Joe, hanging his head, looks up through his mass of curls to his dad.*)

Joe – I'm sorry, Dad.

Gerry – It's all right, son.

Pat – All right??! All right??! How can it be all right?! Look at them!!!

Gerry – The photos are mine, Pat. I'm gay.

(*Pat faints as the curtain falls.*)

# THE PUZZLE

Eileen loved a puzzle. She'd always loved them since she was a little girl. Jigsaws were her favourite then, twenty pieces at first, with a handle on each bit to help small hands guide them into place. She liked pictures of animals and farmyards the best, as she lived up the road from a dairy farm and used to be taken to see the cows being milked. She'd sit on an old stool and watch while the animals came in from the field, marvelling at the size of them all and yearning for the spring when the calves would be born. She loved their little faces with those big dark eyes and nice long lashes and dearly wanted one as a pet, but her mum had said no and the farmer just laughed. "They're hard work," he'd say, but she just couldn't see it as they seemed so obedient and docile. One day, she hoped, she would have one of her own.

As time went on and Eileen went to school, the jigsaws grew larger and more involved. She'd graduated now to 500 pieces and maps of Africa and the British Isles that would stand her in good stead for her geography homework and in knowing whether Chester was north of Birmingham.

Jigsaws, she found, were all-consuming and she happily spent hours each day looking for pieces where nothing seemed to fit, excited when it finally came together, and the overall picture matched that on the box. The sky was always the worst, she thought, trying to match puffballs of cloud and with the shades of blue all looking the same. A good time waster, her mother used to say, as it frequently stopped her from tidying her room, so absorbed was Eileen in her work of art and in securing the elusive final piece.

She went from there to a thousand pieces and could have progressed to so much more if she'd had a table large enough. At least the choice of puzzle grew, from the pieces that were cut in whimsical shapes to the challenging lack of colour variation, as in a snowy scene or forest full of trees.

The older that Eileen found herself, the more the need for puzzles grew, not only as a means of relaxation but as a way of keeping her mind good and active. She also liked riddles that could make her think as she tried to follow the longer and more difficult word games set out as poems or literary charades, popular in the eighteenth century and no less pleasing now.

She really enjoyed a mystery too, if well written with hidden clues, especially an Agatha Christie who led you down a certain path only for you later to find it was full of red herrings and you were chasing the wrong suspect. Miss Christie did this every time and that was her true success. It wasn't always the butler who did it and, just when you found you were sure of his innocence, he turned out guilty after all and only Miss Marple or Poirot knew it. Mysteries, it seemed, were like her jigsaws – you looked at all the pieces therein and tried to find how they fitted together.

The real puzzle was still to come, one of life's mysteries, a real conundrum that sought Eileen out when she first left home and remained a challenge for the rest of her days: how to change a duvet cover. Nothing was hard till she encountered this, not the jigsaws, the riddles or even Sudoku, which she'd never really been able to fathom, having always been better with words than numbers.

Why had this never been taught at school and why wasn't it part of the National Curriculum? Far more use than learning algebra with its odd linear and quadratic equations and more of a life skill than mathematical formulae could ever possibly claim to be. So thought Eileen as she prepared to tackle this problem once more.

A friend was staying, for just the one night, the second guest in less than a week, passing through like ships in the night and leaving her two new puzzles to solve: need she change the cover at all and, if she must, how would she do it? Guest number one had not been dirty but the night creams she used had rubbed on the cover, leaving a smell and a small round stain. Guest number two would surely notice, being something of the sensitive kind who would not take kindly to second-hand linen and not think highly of her friend if she couldn't perform such a simple service for an old and cherished childhood chum. Simple, however, it really was not, as Eileen struggled time and again.

Wishing she'd never progressed from blankets, she threw the duvet on the bed, straightening it out and flattening corners, in serious preparation for the task ahead. Next came the cover, neatly ironed, as plain colours showed the creases more and white was the choice for the bed that night. No one she knew still ironed their linen, but Eileen felt she must take the trouble if the duty had to be done at all.

Taking a corner, left then right, Eileen stalked her intended prey, staring it down like a cheetah with a gazelle. If she acted quickly, she would catch it unawares and lessen the chance of a desperate struggle.

Grabbing the cover inside out, she rolled and pushed, pushed and rolled, sealed end back, sealed end forth, turning the corners right side out and shaking it hard for all she was worth. Wrestling now, at the foot of the bed, Eileen and her exhausted quarry, both dishevelled, both deranged, torn apart by grasping talons.

Muscles pulled and bodies strained, the fight began to reach its end. Neither having won the battle, both collapsed in a unified heap, limbs entwined and sheets all twisted, worse than when it had all begun.

Eileen pondered on this problem, the greatest puzzle of them all. Nothing fitted and nothing completed, the gap in the cover defiant still. Life at the farm had not prepared her. It was easier to milk the cow.

# A HOME OF THEIR OWN

Nellie knew this wasn't for her, the moment she stepped inside the hall. The residents sat around as if waiting for the dentist and a smell of mass cooking pervaded the air. Corridors led in different directions to separate chambers with names on the doors and photos beneath. Photos to show who the occupants were or to guide you back to your cell if confused, as very confused most of them were. They tried to make it nice, of course, but Nellie knew it just wasn't home. Home didn't have a receptionist's desk or people wandering aimlessly, all day and all night, from room to room. Nellie knew this wasn't for her. They even locked the door at night so none of the inmates could ever escape, but Nellie knew she wanted out and Nellie knew she'd find a way.

A mile away, in a small square cage, a howl went up, piercing the night. Charlie the mongrel voiced his pain, loud and clear and all alone. Nobody listened and nobody came, night after night after night after night. It was much the same throughout the day, nobody heeding his plaintive cries, nobody coming to take him away. Other dogs came and went, tails all wagging, waving goodbye, but Charlie stayed just where he was, sad and lonely and giving up hope. Three years he had been in this place, having been found in a local park, tied to a bench, alone without food. Charlie was dumped, unloved, unwanted, left in the open in pouring rain. The other dogs were pedigrees, but Charlie was what they called a "bitsa" – bitsa this, bitsa that, a scruffy little dog with a heart of gold, dark eyes and a keen wet nose. His carers tried to do their best, bringing him meals, throwing him balls, but Charlie knew he didn't belong and yearned for a home of his very own.

Such were the thoughts of Nellie too, three days into residential care. She'd gone from a house to a single room, a small, square space like Charlie's cage. Just like the dog, she wanted to howl, not to end her days like this. She didn't feel old and she didn't feel ill and knew that she could take care of herself. Her doctor had just been overzealous in finding a place at her daughter's request. A round peg in a square hole, Nellie determined to get her house back before it had even been put on the market.

The following day, Nellie acted, setting in train a course of events.

Charlie, meanwhile, lay in his cage, head on his paws, refusing to move. Nothing and no one could interest Charlie and none of the visitors seemed to want him. They all went for fancy new dogs like cockapoos and labradoodles or purebreds and the old-fashioned type. Even the corgi was back in fashion but Charlie the mongrel had no regal blood, just his charms to recommend him: a little mutt with unruly fur, shortish legs and a gentle heart. So much love he had to give, if only someone could see it in him.

As she left the home for the final time, Nellie spotted a little sign, stuck to the glass of the local bus shelter: HOMES WANTED FOR RESCUE DOGS. Nellie had never had a pet but wondered if this could be a new start. A furry friend to keep her company, make her happy, share her days. A smallish dog would be ideal, one to sit upon her lap, snooze together in the afternoons. Everyone should have a friend and Nellie set out to find one.

Taking a nap on the floor of his cage, Charlie dreamt he had found a home. Not wanting to wake from his beautiful dream, he was roused nonetheless by approaching feet and opened his eyes to see who it was. An elderly lady with a kindly face looked at him lovingly and called his name. So many times he'd been here before that Charlie barely raised his head. He couldn't face rejection again and couldn't risk any more heartache.

Nellie opened the door of his cage and bent to stroke his curly head. Her fingers tickled his little ears, her eyes smiling as he began to respond. Minutes later, she picked him up, cuddled him into her ample bosom, kissed him fondly on the head. At that moment, Charlie knew, knew that he was loved at last.

Later that week, in his new home, Charlie explored his

new surroundings. A cosy fire, a nice warm bed and bowls that even had his name on. Charlie certainly loved his food and Nellie loved the crunching of biscuits as, head down, he soon tucked in, making himself quickly at home. For the last three years, his food had seemed tasteless, but Charlie was like a gourmet now, savouring every mouthful given, watched by a clearly delighted Nellie. Charlie didn't want a lot but knew he'd landed on his paws. His owner, Nellie, loved him dearly and loved to watch him run about, for he looked so happy in their garden, sniffing the plants and watering the flowers.

Every day was a new adventure, Charlie and Nellie inseparable now. Indoors or out, they were always together, sitting, playing and having fun. All that they did, they did together, happy and warm in each other's company, fitting together hand in glove. Where one went, the other went too, when one was poorly, the other one knew. A comfort to each other now, a closer pair you couldn't find.

Gone was the cage of Charlie's nightmare, gone was Nellie's single room. Instead, a portrait on the wall depicted the two as everyone saw them – not just belonging but belonging together, even up on the bed at night.

# TO HAVE AND TO HOARD

*It is a truth universally acknowledged, that a single man in possession of a good fortune must be in want of a wife.*[1]

That may have been the case in 1813, thought Gwinnie, but the opposite held true today, some 200 plus years later. It had been her experience when dealing with single men – or women for that matter – that those in possession of a good fortune preferred to hang on to it. This was true of those born into large wealth and certainly of those who'd acquired it (more so, if anything). Gwinnie could give you numerous examples from celebrities to statesmen, from her personal life to her erstwhile career.

She remembered her first job, in the office at the county museum, and the efforts her boss had made to give her important duties that she could later elaborate on when compiling her new CV. He even gave her a proper title for buying the weekly tea and biscuits – Manager of the Tea Club! A pity he gave her nothing more, for when Gwinnie collected the funds each week, she noted he was the last to

---

1  Jane Austen: Pride and Prejudice

pay up, his pockets always seemingly empty. The rest of the team paid on time, their monies recorded in a book and the coins deposited in a tin, locked in the safe overnight. Gwinnie looked at her record book and felt that something had to be done. Her boss was not just short of change (always, every day of the week), but also was the highest-paid – and the one who ate and drank the most. Several cups of tea a day with his hand never out of the biscuit barrel.

Gwinnie watched her boss come in and stride to the tea point behind her desk. She steeled her nerves and rattled her tin, saying his payments were overdue. The same old excuse fell from his lips, that he hadn't any change this week, as he fumbled in his trouser pockets, careful not to jangle the coins. Gwinnie asked if he had any notes, as his debts had gone beyond loose change and – quick as a flash – when she saw his wallet, Gwinnie tore the cash from his hand, promising now to put him in credit.

Those who had money – and her boss was one of them – always seemed to cling to their wealth, whilst the poorest-paid contributed generously to leaving presents and retirement do's, to charity fundraisers – and the weekly tea fund.

Her boss, Gwinnie knew, had once been married – to a stunner of a woman, some had said – but out of the blue, he'd gone and left her, citing extravagant spending habits. He resented the fact that she used his money – his half from their joint account! – while never dipping into her own, piling it up like a modern-day Scrooge.

Those with money always want more but what in the world do they do with it all? There are only so many yachts you can buy and if you haven't got sea legs, they're pointless anyway. Gwinnie's boss didn't have a yacht as he never liked to spend his money. He liked to acquire it, watch it grow, keep it to himself and never share it. What did he do with it, Gwinnie wondered, save worry lest he lose it all.

It was interesting too, how Gwinnie's boss dressed, inside the office as well as out. On the shabby side of casual he looked, though he could well afford a Savile Row suit. All part of the ploy to make him look penniless while secretly hoarding immeasurable wealth. Unlike the gentlemen in Jane Austen's day, who dressed immaculately to attract a wife and were generally very successful in doing so, willing to lavish their wealth upon them and make for a happy ending. So not the case with our modern Mr Bingley, a single man married to his money, professing aloud his wedding vows:

"To have and to hoard, from this day forth."

# DIFFERENT PERSPECTIVES

HELEN

The night was closing in now, the fog forming a shroud around her body as she inched along the towpath, careful not to fall in. It was usually the quickest way home, but not tonight when she couldn't see the path in front of her and the everyday landmarks were clothed in a dark, grey mantle. She was sure she'd walked in the right direction but if that were the case, she'd be home by now. It shouldn't have taken this long.

Helen started to shiver. She had no sense of where she was, and her eyes could make out nothing. She stopped for a moment and looked around but was hit by a wall of fog. She knew she shouldn't have come this way, but she hadn't stopped to think. It was dangerous at the best of times and standing there now in the cold night air, like the blind without a stick, Helen felt totally helpless. She felt like her eyes had been sealed forever, never to open again and, in this strange new world, Helen felt afraid, her heart beating faster with every passing minute.

Resigning herself to moving on, for she couldn't stand

on the spot all night, Helen sighed and shuffled forward, feet scraping along the ground as if too heavy to be lifted up. Unable to see, she felt off balance, swaying a little with every step but trying to keep in a dead straight line for fear of falling into the water.

Something ran across her foot and Helen started, losing her footing and toppling over, right on the very edge of the canal. Stopping herself from falling in, Helen tried to catch her breath, aware of the fate that nearly claimed her, glad of the path that kept her aloft. Rolling across to the other side, to keep her distance from the water, she lay in shock for several minutes, alone and cold and close to tears. Her clothes were very wet and muddy from the uneven path pitted with puddles, a remnant of the rain from the previous week.

Helen blamed Tony for this, as she tended to blame him for everything. He was the one who'd started their row – he was the one who always did. She wished she'd stayed at home that night, then she wouldn't be in this mess right now. He always thought he knew it all, always thought he was in the right and now he'd let her walk home alone, at night, in the dark, in a swirling fog.

Helen clambered to her feet, sore, cold and miserable. Her clothes were torn, her self-esteem battered, but her anger at Tony mustered her courage as she staggered on through the gloom. The sounds of the night were distant yet, her steps the only noise she could hear, reminding her she was all alone.

A sudden flapping of pigeon wings roused her from her idle reverie, her senses alert now to every sound, to every change in atmosphere. A gentle cooing echoed ahead, disturbing the quiet of the night-time air and making her feel she had company at last.

Her eyes straining to see ahead, the night seemed to grow darker still, ink black replacing the grey. With no warning, she cracked her head as the start of the tunnel reared in front of her. Blood trickled down her face and she thought she was going to faint. Helen tried to steady herself, but her hand couldn't grip the slimy surface as the wall dripped down the side of the tunnel.

She started to think of Tony now, warm and dry and safe indoors while she looked forward to the tube ahead of her and the fetid and acrid smell within.

Dizzying thoughts pervaded her mind as she fought to maintain her consciousness. She hoped her eyes would adjust to the dark and end this nightmare she found herself in. Drawing her body into itself, Helen tried to keep herself warm, not caring now how she looked since no one was there to see her. In this dank, unfriendly space, she stumbled on precariously with little idea of time or place.

Gradually the tunnel came to an end, taking her wretched journey with it. The fog began to clear at last and Helen could stump her weary way home, broken, dishevelled and longing for rest.

Opening the door she flicked the switch, the light at

once gracing her little room, sending greetings of joy across her flat and towards her sad and bloodied face. Helen lay down on the welcome settee, filthy and sore but at peace at last.

TONY

Tony couldn't concentrate. He should never have let her go alone. Not in the state she was in. She sure was mad at him. Again. Every week he invited her over for a meal and every week she came. She knew no one else in London and London was a big place.

His little sister Helen. Newly arrived and in a new job. "Knowing nothing and no one" was how she'd put it, which was why he was trying to help her. Eight years his junior, Helen was twenty. Just out of school in Tony's book and wet behind the ears. Her big brother would help her, for he was worldly-wise.

The evening had started well, as every week it did. Helen came straight from work, to find Tony in the kitchen, chef's apron on, glass of wine in his hand. Skate with black butter was on the menu, a dish that Tony cooked well. It was hard to find skate wings these days, but Tony knew a local man who could always secure them – at a price.

Helen watched as the capers went in, amazed at her brother's culinary skills. He seemed to have a certain panache, a *"Je ne sais quoi"* as the French would say. Helen could scarcely boil an egg, so was glad of her weekly invitation and the chance to sample Tony's cooking. Many a girl had been entertained with his *crêpes suzette au curaçao* or *canard à l'orange* or *truites aux amandes*. He certainly knew how to wine and dine and could have made a living at it if he hadn't gone into carpentry.

Helen had inherited none of this talent and was neither practical nor academic. So far, she'd just drifted along in life, riding on the waves of her brother's success, doing and wanting nothing in particular. It hadn't really mattered as yet but now she was in London, in a rented flat, and Helen had started to think. The thought of excitement had brought her to town, but she'd found none yet as it was all too expensive or far away. Her sense of direction was pretty poor, and the underground map had left her bewildered.

Tony had taught her the route to his flat, there and back several times, till firmly imprinted on her brain. He'd even drawn her a little diagram, with the canal marked on it and pictures of trees, to help when walking there on her own. So far so good, Tony thought, but tonight he would rip it up in front of her, to force her not to rely on aids.

Brother and sister enjoyed their meal and settled down to their usual chat. Tony's work was going well, with five new orders for cabinets and a bigger job that would last some months, restoring the pews at the local church with a chance to carve his own designs.

Helen, meanwhile, was employed in an office, learning how to use a spreadsheet, a job she found boring and uneventful. The Excel formulae made no sense, and she couldn't see the point of it anyway. She didn't know what she wanted to do but she knew it wasn't an office job if spreadsheets were all they had to offer.

Tony opened another bottle, the wine helping their conversation, till the subject of money reared its head. He thought she should go for a different job, one that would better pay her bills and give her a greater interest in life. He, after all, had done so well, had learnt a trade and was successful at it. He thought she should try and learn a skill, take evening classes to help with her job. In time she could work her way up the ladder, seek promotion, reach the top. She really ought to make more effort, in her profession and also her personal life. She'd never had a relationship and who indeed would take her on, content as she was to mump on others, happy to drift along in their wake. Helen needed to sort herself out and not rely on him so much.

Helen listened to Tony's spiel, anger rising from deep within her. How dare he talk to his sister like this when she'd come to him for support and comfort. He knew that she had no one else, he knew she wasn't blessed with talent. Why did he have to interfere, upset the evening yet again. Every week it came to this, every week he prattled on. Why could he not mind his own business and stop telling her what to do. Every week he started a row, every week ended like this. She wasn't asking him for money, she hadn't asked to come to his flat. She should never have come here tonight. Let him keep his skate and wine and find someone else to entertain. Helen had had enough of it.

Grabbing her coat from the peg in the hall, Helen reached inside the pocket, her hand locating the well-worn map, her trusty assistant to find her way home. She smoothed it out to check the route as Tony bolted from his seat, grabbing the piece of paper from her and tearing it up before her eyes.

Helen stared in utter horror, thinking what her next move should be. She had to leave, that much was clear, after such a destructive scene. Slamming the door with all her might, Helen left the flat that night, just as a fog began to descend. She had to find her own way home without the help of her faithful guide, in pieces now on her brother's floor.

Tony sat amongst the debris of dirty plates and empty glasses. Helen would surely find her way home. It wasn't far and she'd been before. Twenty minutes would probably do it, if she kept to the way she always came, and the path was lit – in places at least. He shouldn't worry, he really shouldn't. Helen would soon be safe indoors, feet up and watching the telly. He'd call tomorrow and make amends, ask her over for a meal next week and start the cycle off again.

# THE GRASS IS ALWAYS GREENER

Trish's head was full of dreams. Awake or asleep, transported away, her mind in another zone. In bed at night, she drifted off into a world apart from the one she lived in – a better place she liked to think, a happier place than the one that was real to her. She liked to go to sleep and dream, to dwell in a house that wasn't her own, with roses round the door and birds in the garden, in a road called Donkey Lane. It was much the same as her daytime imaginings, when she looked out the window of her high-rise flat overlooking the Blackwall Tunnel and the heavy traffic waiting to enter it. If she opened the window, she could smell the fumes when all she wanted to smell was grass and the delicate scent of hyacinths. She hadn't even a balcony, nowhere to put a plant or two, nowhere to grow a few tomatoes or watch and wait for her seeds to come up. Trish could only sit and dream as she looked at the cars trundling by, commuters on their way to work.

In one of those cars sat Patrick Moynahan, fingers drumming on the steering wheel. He took this journey every day from his home to his office and back again. Hour upon hour in the same queue, over and over and over again, looking at other frustrated drivers, revving their engines and desperate to move. There they sat, radios on, numbed by the chatter and daily news, rarely listening to what was said, immune to the usual depressing stories. It was noise in the background as they sat and waited, along with the blaring horns outside. If only Patrick could give up work, retire early and move to the sea and never have to commute again.

In the car in front sat Mike and Penny, father and daughter and anxious both. The time on the clock was ticking away as Penny fretted and bit her nails. Half an hour till her interview and she wondered if she would ever make it. She knew they'd left in plenty of time but hadn't envisaged a broken-down truck and a single file of snail-like traffic. Her father was ever the optimist but even he was looking worried as he stared ahead at the queue in front. Mike knew what it meant to Penny – her first job after school and one she really wanted to have. Her head was full of the stage and screen and a theatre post was up for grabs, one where she'd meet all the famous stars.

For Olivia though, the glamour was fading, as she left for rehearsals once again. She'd wanted to act from an early age, to tread the boards, to hear the applause, but it hadn't quite worked out that way and every day was sheer hard graft, with early mornings and little money. Half the year was usually resting and often ended on the fringe or repeating plays in repertory, a constant round of learning lines with never an Oscar or Tony in sight. If only Olivia had more money, she'd set up her own theatre company, produce good plays and act the lead. She'd also have a holiday, which she hadn't done in fourteen years. She'd love to jet off to the sun, find a man on Bondi Beach, marry him by the rolling waves and dance till midnight on the sand.

That had long been Shelley's dream before her man had up and left her, even before their wedding day. He'd run off with her once best friend, leaving her stranded in Sydney Harbour without her ticket home again. She'd love to find a genuine man, one who was kind, caring and true, but at her age they were hard to come by and often came with kids in tow. Not that she minded kids at all but she'd prefer to have had her own from birth. Perhaps she'd buy a dog instead, a faithful companion, loyal and good, one who would honour and obey, keep her company through the night.

Just like Sophie, who'd wanted a dog but ended up with fish instead. She'd often fancied a little mutt, a furry friend to share her days, a new best friend, a canine chum, someone to ease her loneliness, someone to give her a purpose in life and join her on her daily run. She'd gone one day to the rescue place and could have really bought them all, their sad eyes tugging her heartstrings, begging her to take them home. But Sophie hadn't considered the cost and left the centre empty-handed. She'd have to have another think, work out what her plan would be. A friend suggested tropical fish, lots of variety and soothing to watch but Sophie couldn't choose which ones and opted instead for three young goldfish, naming them Goldie, Dolly and Fred. They swam about in their tank all day, while Sophie went out on her usual run without a doggy friend beside her.

Andrew Scott would have liked a run, being disabled and in a chair. He'd once been a famous distance runner till fate had put an end to that. A speeding motorist, out of the blue, had knocked him down and injured his legs, forcing him never to walk again. His life had changed in other ways too and he knew he'd have to learn to adapt. His car had been altered to allow him to drive and he'd hired a man to tend his garden, but he never felt that it looked the same and he soon grew tired of instructing him. What he'd like was a nice little flat, with minimal effort and a pleasant view. He'd have swapped his house with Trish's flat – if only it hadn't been full of fumes!

# GETTING TO KNOW YOU

Unusually for a Monday, it had all been going so well. First, Molly's train had been on time after weeks of frustration caused by faulty signalling outside London Bridge. Then her talk on the history and development of penicillin as a result of mycological research had been so successful as to achieve a standing ovation from an enthusiastic audience at the Wellcome. How Alexander Fleming must have felt at his accidental discovery, way back in 1928, was something Molly could only marvel at, though she had felt his excitement earlier as she answered question after question from a group of young scientists.

It was two hours later, on attempting to leave the building, that the day had started to unravel. She had entered the lift on the top floor with a man she'd recognised from her talk, a tall, good-looking man with blond spiky hair, who'd sat at the back taking copious notes. Nothing was said between them as the lift door closed and they began their descent. No eye contact was made, as is usual when people who don't know each other travel in a lift together. The same can be said for dentists' waiting rooms or sitting on a bus, unless you're of a certain age and actively looking for someone to talk to. That happens often with the elderly, with those who live on their own and those with no family and sometimes no friends. The bus becomes a temporary social club and allows them to pass the time of day and a few thoughts with a random stranger in a way that seldom happens when you're young and embarrassed to speak to anybody for fear that they might reply.

Molly stared straight ahead, with an occasional glance from the corner of her eye at the spiky haired stranger standing beside her. He stared too, down at his shoes (scuffed and dirty), up at the ceiling (discoloured and worn). Each had a feeling of slight embarrassment, as is common when a silence goes on too long between people who barely know each other and struggle for what to say. Molly didn't know him at all, save that he was in her class that day. At least he'd heard her speak, so knew her voice and love of her subject, knew her name and why she was there.

Those seconds in silence seemed to lengthen as the pair descended and the quiet remained, until abruptly and without warning, the lift jerked to a sudden and violent halt. Its occupants glanced at each other quickly, uncertain what was to happen next, until Molly started pressing buttons, one at a time, then frantically, willing her actions to take effect. She let out a sigh as nothing happened, the lift remaining obstinate and still. "It's stuck" she said, stating the obvious and breaking the silence for the very first time

"Yes" he replied, pressing the alarm, economical with words but taking command. Molly wished she'd done that first before striking out at every button in sheer frustration at having stopped. Surely they must have reached the ground and the door would open shortly.

As the clock ticked on and the alarm was pressed a few more times, Molly hammering on the lift door with added urgency and increasing desperation, the reluctant companions began to realise they were in for the long haul, and they'd better hunker down until rescue came.

Molly sat down on her overnight bag, grateful that she was staying at a friend's and pleased it was packed with both clothes and books, raising her somewhat off the lift floor. At the multistorey, the lifts reeked of pee, used as a handy night-time urinal by those who couldn't quite make it home or those who simply didn't care. A powerful disinfectant often added to the smell, penetrating the nostrils and contributing to the stench in an unsuccessful attempt at sweetness and cleanliness. Thank heavens for the cleaners of the Wellcome Trust who kept their lift in a better state!

Incarcerated in her cell, with no way out and the solitary light dim, Molly looked at the four lift walls and wished there was something more she could do. She watched a fly, as helpless as she, going round in circles, searching for air, seeming occasionally to twiddle its thumbs but really keeping its body clean. Not a lot she could do on that score herself, save pray her confinement ended soon.

A sudden hand thrust in her face reminded her she was not alone. "Gary," said the voice beside her, close within her prison walls. Jolted out of her trance-like state, mind numb and all a blur, Molly stood to face her inmate, having weirdly forgotten he was even there. "Hi," said Molly, "Molly Keene. When do you think we'll be released?" Gary laughed and countered back: "Not till the parole board's met next Tuesday!"

"Better be on good behaviour then" quipped Molly to her newfound friend, "or I'll be gone, and you'll be left, another ten-stretch waiting for you!" The cellmates laughed and bantered on, enjoying each other's repartee as minutes lengthened into hours with neither aware of the passing time.

A suggestion was made to play I-spy, but the game petered out after few attempts and creative use of the imagination. There were only so many words for walls, and all had been used at the start of the game, foreign vocabulary disallowed.

Hide-and-seek was Gary's suggestion, more as a way to make Molly laugh, the reality offering little scope unless he could hide in Molly's bag! They looked around at their intimate space, glad there were only two of them in it, so small was the area they found themselves in. Imagine the lift at full capacity with nowhere to move and nowhere to hide! Be grateful for small mercies, they thought – there might be an obnoxious bore in that crowd!

They longed for freedom and open space – the flat, arid tableland of Patagonia or the untamed Pampas of Argentina. Either would be ideal right now, however difficult the climate.

Molly had noted on other occasions how adversity could bring out the best in people. Some had called it the "wartime spirit" even when referring to minor events. While waiting for trains that were delayed or cancelled, Molly had witnessed a coming-together in a combined spirit of comradeship, of people previously unknown to each other, who had never spoken before in their lives, even when seeing each other daily on the same spot on the same platform. Suddenly they felt they had something in common and were willing to share it with each of their neighbours, chewing over the state of the railways. The same had occurred when needing to spend a penny and nobody had the right change or when caught in the rain and the shelter was closed. Strangers suddenly wanted to chat, to share the experience with a fellow sufferer. Such was happening with Molly and Gary, who'd never met before today and would possibly never meet again unless Gary came to another talk. He might indeed be prompted then to raise his hand and ask a question, rather than sit in the shadows at the back, taking down her every word for quiet consumption later on.

Not before time their rescuers came, releasing both from

their shared ordeal and sending them out into the night, Molly off to her worried friend, Gary home to cook a meal. Each had enjoyed the other's company, agreeing then to meet again soon – at ground level with no need of a lift. At the Wellcome they'd use the stairs in future!

# DECLUTTERING

Why did her house always look so cluttered? Not to her it didn't but it's what people always said when they came. Not that they came often but when they did it's what they said. She was always being told she had too much "stuff" – too many books, too many ornaments, too many everything. She didn't think so herself and to her – Bridget – it looked homely, lived-in, cosy. It was how a home *should* look if it was to be called a home and not a house and she liked to have her possessions around her. All of them.

It had not been the same at work. Bridget took pride in her tidy desk and colleagues had often commented on it. A laptop, a phone and a cup of tea were her only office adornments. Not for her the potted plants, photos of family and bags of crisps. A tidy desk was a tidy mind and cleared her head for the tasks of the day. It was also a way of separating out, of making a distinction between home and office. The two, for Bridget, were very different worlds and such they had always remained. Work was business, home was home, somewhere to relax and snuggle into, a comfort outside office hours.

As she sat with a steaming cup of tea, feet on the sofa, resting on cushions, Bridget reached for the remote control. She sighed as she switched from channel to channel, trying to find something interesting. She flicked through the usual endless array of cookery programmes and gardening shows, of popular quizzes and daily soaps, till her thumb stopped pressing the keys at last as she landed on a reality show. Not her usual type of viewing but Bridget was drawn to the male presenter, urging a woman to empty her home or at least reduce it by fifty per cent. It seemed he thought she had too much in it and ought to dispose of half of her "stuff" regardless of whether she liked it or not. The poor woman was close to tears as her teenage daughters egged her on, begging their mum to modernise and throw away what she didn't need. They felt she'd be so much happier if every room was cleared of "junk". There'd be less to dust and lots more space, though their mum didn't seem at all convinced as she looked around at her lifetime's work. It had taken years to gather these jewels, and each had its own story to tell. It was, she felt, like a little museum, with pieces acquired over time and she their devoted and loyal curator.

Bridget scoffed at the daughters' pleas to make their mum a minimalist. It tended to be the trend these days, to live in a much simpler style, though Bridget thought it cold and spartan. Why would she want so much space when it made the rooms seem soulless and empty? Better by far to live as she did than to sit like a prisoner in a cell.

Yet the pressure was on to minimalise, to create effect by a few possessions rather than crowd out every surface. Less is more, or so it was said, if you had the courage to eliminate. Removing the unnecessary from your life would free you up to what really mattered and help you focus on what was of value. It was meant to be good for your mental health, to give less stress in your daily life, to provide clarity instead of chaos and allow for a happier way of being.

Bridget didn't hold with this zen way of life and thought instead it had something lacking. She'd heard of the scientific reports that suggested clutter disrupted focus and gave you a feeling of overload. But Bridget had never felt that way and couldn't see what the fuss was about. What was clutter anyway? To some it smacked of gross disorder, but Bridget knew where everything was, and all was in its rightful place. Her friends said her house felt claustrophobic, like the walls were closing in around them, but Bridget's eye saw only comfort in every corner of the room. They called her a hoarder, but she challenged this and said she was rather a fine collector, a purveyor who dealt in particular goods. Never mind if she *needed* this "stuff", she *wanted* it for a number of reasons and wanting – to her – was reason enough.

Clearing your home and clearing your mind, to Bridget only left you bereft. Both, to her, were a treasure trove, full of richness and quality, amassed over time and carefully tended like plants in a soil that grew in their beauty. To cut them back would be a sacrilege, an act of extreme vandalism. Many, she knew, had trodden this path and lived to rue the very day, missing that which had given them pleasure, leaving a hollow and gaping chasm.

Open and sparse, for some, may have merits but Bridget knew what she would choose.

# THE CEMETERY

Why did they do it? It was so insensitive. Building a care home opposite a cemetery so the residents could see their next move. It was the same with hospitals. The patients could look out of the window and view their future home if their surgery was unsuccessful. Distasteful. Quiet a cemetery may be but so is an open field or a nice little wooded area with birds singing in the trees and the sun poking through the leaves. Much more pleasant, surely.

It was not like they could watch the world go by, unless you counted the funeral corteges, one after another throughout the day, so slowly they'd send you to sleep. Like counting sheep but less attractive and not what you'd call people-watching, though it was always interesting to see the fashions. Black these days was out of vogue, with mourners dressed in varying colours, the brighter the better it sometimes seemed. Not so much a sad goodbye but a celebration of life, it was said. Heaven knows where this could lead to – a throwing of hats in the air or dancing around the deceased person's grave. If only the dead were there to enjoy it.

Some people liked a cemetery, of course. That poet for instance: Thomas Grave. No, Gray. Thomas Gray. He wrote about a country churchyard, didn't he. Not sure what else he wrote but that was a good one. It rhymed and everything. Come to think of it, not entirely sure whether he liked all those graves or not. It's a beautiful elegy but muses on death as the fate of us all. A bit of a leveller, that.

Wandering around on a summer's day, with bees and butterflies in the air, a gentle breeze caressing the face, a cemetery seems a peaceful place. The graves themselves will often vary, from family vaults to single cells, from worn-out stones to fresh new mounds, each with its own characteristics. Some well-tended, some neglected, forgotten or abandoned over the years, the sleepers within constant throughout. Deep within their earthy homes, active no more but living and breathing in their day and people just like us.

For the Victorians, of course, it was a good day out, visiting the relatives and enjoying a meal. What better place for a bite to eat than seated around a loved one's grave, blanket on the ground, picnic at the ready. Cheese and pickle, anyone?

The cemetery was a place of comfort and, before the influx of public parks, laid out like gardens or a mini paradise, with ponds and pathways and a proper landscape. Smaller churchyards began to give way to burial grounds with a larger capacity, following outbreaks of cholera and yellow fever and a dramatic rise in the population.

Welcome then the Magnificent Seven, London's answer to overcrowding, skirting the city as Victorian gothic garden cemeteries, beautifully planted with trees and shrubs. A rich history is shared between them, and each has a fascinating story, from the coffin lifts and underground chambers to the notable burials and exhumations. Home to the wealthy, the pauper, the famous, to believers, the faithful and non-conformists, the Magnificent Seven was a place to be seen – a pity you had to be dead to achieve it.

Most of the Seven fell into decline, their gothic splendour engulfed by nature early on in the twentieth century. Home still to original residents, the gardens gradually turned to woodland, dense shrubs overwhelming the stones, slowly becoming a haven for wildlife and creating a spectral and ethereal scene. By day or by night, the sites can seem eerie, with unwelcome shadows and rustling of leaves. Never, it seems, walking alone, as the ghosts of the dead hover within, watching and waiting while remaining unseen. Their slumbers woken by the passage of feet, in, over and around their graves, as many a tomb is now unseen, covered in tendrils from encroaching trees.

Step forth then, the Friends of the cemeteries, clearing ivy, cutting grass, sprucing up the many pathways, working together, learning a craft. Join them in the summer season, fun days held within the park, have an ice cream, bring your picnic, rest your head upon a stone. Get to know the social history, the older characters dwelling there, marvel at the wondrous beauty – and order your crushed avocado roll.

# THE SUET BALL CHALLENGE

How it had all changed. When she'd started work all those years ago, it had been so different. People had fun then, Lucy thought – at work. They put the hours in, of course, and were assiduous in their duties but they also had time for a laugh. It wasn't like that now. Her colleagues were too busy to look up from their desks, ate their lunch where they sat and had no time for banter or casual chat. No wonder they were stressed.

Lucy had always been good at her job and rose through the ranks to a senior post, but she'd always maintained a healthy balance and friends around her saw it paid off. Always one for a laugh and a joke, Lucy was the mistress of the office party, metaphorically only, that is, being happily married at twenty-five. She was also renowned for numerous pranks and had often been seen in fancy dress, sitting in on a Trustees' meeting as if tutu and tiara were her usual attire. She could certainly not get away with that now but at the time it was thought of as humorous, and she'd often repeated the act in a different disguise.

Lucy was popular with the less senior staff, for her

fairness as a line manager and her thoughtful and caring nature but just as much so for her irrepressible sense of fun, which brightened their every day. It was a joy to come into work each week and they always gave their best for Lucy.

Colleagues recalled, one summer afternoon, the announcement of a new event and one in which they were all to take part – the orange bowling championships. Each took an orange from the communal bowl and stood by their desks awaiting instruction. Lucy appeared, as *maître d'*, dressed in a black tuxedo jacket and skirt, in kitten heels and waving a wand. She led them out to a long corridor that stretched from their office to the Chief Executive's suite and placed an orange at the furthest end. One at a time they took their turn, rolling their fruit down the carpeted alley, seeing who could hit the target.

The Chief Executive was out that day – or so Lucy thought – before the capers began. As he sat at his desk, writing a report, he was startled to see an orange roll by, on its own at first but then followed by others. One by one the oranges came, some at speed, others slowly, with short intervals in between. Thinking perhaps he'd been working too hard, the Chief Executive rose to his feet and made his way to his office door. An orange pippin rumbled by, a rogue in the bowl of jaffas and navels, met by a chorus of cheers and shrieks as the apple hit its mark spot on.

"Our five a day!" cried Lucy happily as her boss came marching from his room, purposeful steps pounding the floor. "You've missed your turn," cried Lucy again as his face broke into a very broad grin and he reached for a lemon from the bowl. Looking back, they were happy days, times that allowed her to reminisce in this strange and serious businesslike world where nobody smiled and nobody laughed.

Time to have some fun again, thought Lucy as she hatched a plan, sitting at home one winter's afternoon. Resurrect her famous championships, treat them like an Olympic sport, prepare a podium for the worthy winner, but this time with a little twist.

Lucy and her husband were well-known "twitchers" – spending much of their time watching birds and looking for rare sightings, often travelling great distances to do so but also from the comfort of their own home. They spent a fortune on quality food – seeds and peanuts, mealworms and suet – in the hope of attracting a variety of birds and were pleased with their overall general success.

On cold winter mornings, Lucy stood at her door and hurled a suet ball down the garden, to avoid going out in pyjamas and slippers and catching her very death of cold. Over the years her aim had improved, and she no longer hit the garden gnomes or broke the glass in her neighbour's cold frame. She'd gone from winning bronze to gold in her own imaginary Olympic games, admittedly as the only entrant but pleased nonetheless with her consistent performance. Just as much fun as throwing the discus or tossing the caber at the Highland Games, Lucy knew this could gain a following if properly staged and promoted well.

Her sixtieth birthday approaching fast, Lucy invited her friends around, old colleagues from her orange-bowling days. Once they'd had a drink or two – this being a celebratory event – Lucy led them out to the garden, armed with her box of suet balls. At the start of the path, she'd chalked a line, behind which the players would stand, before each in turn would pitch their ball between two posts at the end of the lawn. The aim of the game was to fling the ball as far as one could, in a straight line and damaging nothing – risky after too much wine.

Betty Walsh was disqualified for daring to serve like a tennis pro (an overhand toss disallowed), while Mary Martin's suet crumbled, raining down in greasy specks to be fought over later by angry crows. Alex Coughlan dug her heels in, spinning round for an expert throw, but lost her balance and toppled over, squashing her ball of fat beneath her. Last in line came Phyllis Walker, always one to put on a show. Walking up with pace and precision, Phyllis studied the path ahead. In her mind she measured the distance, trajectory and weight of the ball, before stepping forward to the throwing line and bending as far as her knees would allow. Suet clasped firmly in her hand, Phyllis swung her right arm forward, watching her missile fly through the air, between the posts and up to the fence.

Tumultuous applause shattered the silence as Phyllis straightened up again, then curtseyed to her adoring friends, aware that she had won the game. Lucy led her to the podium, a makeshift platform made of bricks. Upon this rostrum Phyllis stood, a chocolate medal round her neck, a wreath of leaves upon her head. A new Olympic champion crowned, one of five women who'd taken part, joined together like interlocking rings, a commonality amongst them all – to keep the flame of friendship alive and always have fun along the way.

# PENDLE, LANCASHIRE

1692. Salem, Massachusetts. Hordes of men were gathering now, down at the port, brandishing weapons and burning torches. A deadly witch hunt was under way, and these were Puritans, intent on ridding the State of sorcery. The work of the devil must be flushed out, his accomplices made to pay with their lives. Women who didn't conform to society, who'd made a pact with Satan himself; women who didn't adhere to discipline, who ignored the Puritans' strict moral code. It was these that the men were seeking to find, to drag them out of their secret lairs, to torture them and make them confess, then hang them for their guilty deeds.

Bridget and Mary ran for their lives, from the heavy pounding of feet that followed them, closing in with a fevered zeal.

In a hilltop village, over 3,000 miles away, and eighty years on from their own local witch trials, an angry mob had gathered together, on Pendle Hill where the trouble began, way back in 1612. Recent spates of injured livestock, of crops having failed and soured milk, had led to the hunting down of Agnes, a local woman with extraordinary skills, thought to be in league with the devil.

The seventh daughter of a seventh daughter (and of a seventh daughter yet again), Agnes had inherited special powers, able to see into the future, able to heal sickness and administer cures. Her family dwelt in the Forest of Pendle, an untamed and hilly landscape, to the east of the hill from which the village was named. Extreme poverty marked them out and their begging was considered a social problem, as they made their way asking for food in a persistent and immoderate manner.

Objects found around their dwelling had led to suspicions of unsavoury powers. Metal pins, scattered about, were seen as proof of witches' behaviour, together with nails and pieces of felt that were found in stoppered pots and jugs. Clay images were also discovered – a sign of malpractice when partially crumbled – and linked to the harming of several people. Agnes, for many, was the cause of it all and the mob was there to seek her out. They'd hunt her down like a fox chased by hounds and follow her till she could run no more.

It wasn't hard to assemble the mob, so many families afflicted of late. Some had experienced personal injury, seen children have uncontrollable fits, while others watched their folk run mad or suffer lameness as a result of the spells and witchery. The devil's magic was being practised and the villagers wanted an end to it all.

On the moors o'er the village stood Gallows Hill, a reminder of the hangings of 1612, the grisly fate of ten witches accused of murder by supernatural powers. The mob was on the move again, banging pans and shouting charges, carrying flames and branches of rowan to protect against witchcraft and evil enchantment. Their voices grew louder with every step as Agnes was sighted up ahead.

The young woman was out of breath, running for miles on uneven ground. Her heart beat fast within her chest as she tried to flee her revengeful accusers, hard now upon her heels. Her feet ribboned from sharp stones, they blistered and bled as she stumbled on, tripping and falling as she went. Agnes was sick behind a bush as the thought of torture turned her stomach, making her heave and retch a while. She called for help, but nobody came as the mob advanced, closing in. A swarm of anger, gathering pace, moving forward with one intent.

Out of the dark a figure came, clothed in black and blending in. Agnes had no time to think when this shadowy form grabbed her hand, pulling her swiftly to one side and making her crouch upon the ground. He knew her name (which startled her) and whispered in an urgent tone. He'd come to help her get away, escape the fate that summoned her, remove her from this fearful scene. Agnes stared at the man before her, listened to his pleading voice, urging her to come away, far from the tempest surrounding them.

Paralysed through fear and shock, crouching low upon

the ground, Agnes saw the crowds rush past, flaming torches in their hands, shouting her guilt and wishing her dead. She turned to face the form beside her, wondering what his motives were. She'd never seen his face before and questioned why he wanted to help. All around her sought her blood, sought to see her on the gallows. Why should this man be so different, want to save her, set her free?

Firm and gentle all at once, he led her from the baying mob, walking on a path less travelled, slowly and surely through the night. On the way he told his story, of his sister dear and very ill. Death itself had seemed to claim her, all hope shredded on the floor. Yet in their midst had come a woman, elderly and very poor, offering herbs and ancient remedies, resinous substances, healing balms. Applying her knowledge and age-old skills, the hag restored his sister to health, then disappeared into the forest, vanishing from whence she came, never to be seen or heard of again. That woman was young Agnes' grandmother, a village healer, not the devil's aide, the seventh daughter of a seventh daughter, with special powers to cure the sick.

Agnes and the man walked on, for many miles into the night, until they reached a neighbouring county, as the sun came up on a bright new world.

# THE FREEBIES

Mr and Mrs Freeby lived at number 38. It wasn't their real name. It could have been the Robinsons, the Williams or anything else really but Mr and Mrs Freeby is how they were known. Or the Freebies, to those who knew them well. They didn't know that's what they were called and had never heard it said, but Mr and Mrs Freeby was how everyone referred to them. Or the Freebies, as previously mentioned.

The Freebies had a daughter – Mary Sue. She knew about the Freebies but she wasn't one herself and never planned to be one with their cheapskate reputation. She found it too embarrassing when she heard what neighbours said – that her parents paid for nothing (though that wasn't strictly true).

They were never very popular down at their local pub as they never bought a round or even a bag of crisps. The two would stand there watching till a friend was at the bar, then quietly sidle over and perform their usual act. It was by now a well-rehearsed routine, as they tried to look hesitant, deciding what to have, then acted all surprised when someone offered a drink. Friends fell for it every time, largely being embarrassed not to, but cursed themselves later for not holding back and waiting to see what happened. Those moments could seem like hours though, as they all stood at the bar, and it was easier to buy a round than stand in anguish waiting, for the Freebies would never offer – of that they could all be certain. The publican called them "Tired Hands" as they never seemed to move – not in their pockets for cash, though they were quick to pick up a glass.

It wasn't that they were poor. Maybe that was why – because they kept their money to themselves and never spent a penny. Or that was how it seemed as they went to some extremes, like always going to funerals to be sure of a free meal after. They sang in fine voice at any of the chosen hymns, looked dutifully sad and always wore black. It was often wondered how they knew so many people, to be always at the grave, always in mourning clothes, but the Freebies carried on without ever seeming to care as long as they went to the reception after and enjoyed a drink and some tasty, catered food.

They had money, of course they did, but were never keen to spend it, going out of their way to avoid paying for anything.

Members of the National Trust, courtesy of Mary Sue who bought their subscription every year, they certainly made the most of it, going to their local sites several times a month because they knew they could enter for free. It wasn't the houses they were interested in, or even particularly the gardens, but they enjoyed the clean toilets and the nicely smelling soap. They could stay in the café all day, without anyone hurrying them on, nursing the one cup of coffee that they purchased with a voucher. What the Freebies really liked was the free tap water, available all day long and to which they could help themselves. There was no embarrassment here, in going for the umpteenth glass, as they didn't have to ask for it and could just serve themselves. The water was a puzzle to Mary Sue, as her parents didn't like the taste. They were never considered the healthy type and never drank water at home – unless in a glass of whisky. It was simply there to be taken, like the white serviettes and the various sachets, all so appealing in their nice, bright colours. Why they should want a sachet of vinegar or mayonnaise with their glass of water was known by all but challenged by none. The Freebies would load them into their bags without so much as a by-your-leave and nobody said a word.

It was very typical of the couple to take things that weren't even wanted, like cereal bars handed out at the station and other sundry promotional offers. As long as they never had to pay, they took what was offered and went on their way. Some of these "gifts" were later recycled, given away with *grande largesse* as if bestowing a crock of gold, while in reality clearing a cupboard.

The Freebies made an art of it all, doing the rounds of producers' markets, looking for free samples of food to avoid going home and making lunch and basically taking anything going, whether wanted, needed or not. They always took the breakfast rolls, when staying at some swanky hotel, paid for with Mary Sue's hard-earned cash, and not just the rolls but the fillings too, from cold meat and eggs to tomatoes and cheese. If they were allowed to eat it at breakfast time, they saw nothing wrong with scoffing it for lunch. Mary Sue had paid for it after all.

Like the packets of coffee, sugar and tea in their hotel room, along with those little cartons of milk – UHT but free of charge, which they had replenished whenever they could in order to build a proper supply to be taken home at the end of the week. They were only pleased to have cancelled the milkman.

And let's not forget the toiletries! All those wonderful miniatures, the delight of any hotel stay, often arranged in a little basket, with dental floss and shower caps. Mrs Freeby had hundreds of those, though she never remembered using any. Why would she want a shower cap when trying out the new conditioner?

Much was a mystery to Mary Sue, though she wondered if it wasn't an age thing. Her parents seemed to horde this stuff while she was one for minimalism. Did they really save that much by collecting vouchers and abstemious means, or were they just sensibly thrifty? For who *wouldn't* accept a gift if lucky enough to be offered one? Such niceties rarely came her way, and she began to think she might be jealous. It was just that her parents went to extremes and had gained an unenviable reputation.

Mary Sue sat at the bus stop, waiting impatiently for the number 19 and checking she'd brought her debit card with her. She had no idea what her journey would cost as it all went through on contactless. Mary Sue stopped as she caught herself thinking of her wonderful new life ahead and her future (free!) seniors' pass. She was one of the family after all.

# THE SEED

Helena sighed as she looked at the packet before her. Everything was difficult to open these days. Her shrink-wrapped fish was designed to torture. She should have paid more and gone elsewhere but the wet fish shop had closed long ago, and she wasn't sure they'd have sold it anyway. Basa wasn't from around these shores.

She'd never been good at opening *anything*. When she'd shared a flat with a couple of friends, they'd laughed at the way she'd struggled with the milk, mauling the carton like a hungry tiger, leaving it open, unable to close. You were supposed to pull at diagonal corners, performing some kind of wizardry, but Helena didn't have the knack and regularly got covered in milk, much to her friends' eternal delight.

It had all started with the corned beef tin and the little key that opened it up, winding round in a thin line, enclosing itself in fine metal as it circled the top of the tin. As a child, she had often watched her mother, who managed the task effortlessly while issuing warnings to take great care if you wanted to avoid a terrible accident. Helena longed to open a tin as she saw it then as a little game, but she was older now and hopefully wiser, having cut herself on many occasions.

She often wondered how the elderly managed or those on their own with no one to help. It shouldn't be such a difficult job to open a jar of marmalade but, my word, you felt like you'd conquered the world if you managed to prise the lid off the top without the need of a pair of tongs.

Helena put her fish in the fridge for Bill to open when he came home from work. She knew he would open it instantly and not even think how helpless she'd been. He'd pour the drinks while she cooked their tea, and they'd settle down for the evening together.

While she waited, she'd work in the garden, dead head some flowers, tidy the paths. She'd think about what she could plant for the summer and how to fill the gaps with colour. Helena went through her packets of seeds, sorting them out between flowers and herbs, checking the dates for when to sow. She thought they'd have oregano this year and some lettuce and tomatoes for their summer salads.

More packets to open, she thought, though usually easier than opening her fish. They tended to tear across the top and, unless you ripped them in too much haste, generally opened in one straight line. The contents, however, had to be heeded, as some seeds were tiny and numerous within. In Helena's usual, inimitable way, the lot could be scattered across the floor like those pesky cards at Christmas time which people filled with tons of glitter that left you clearing it up for days.

Playing it safe, she reached for the scissors and cut a corner from the shiny packet. Poppy seeds were quite minute, little devils if dropped on the floor, small dark specks that looked like dirt, but which grew to be the most beautiful flowers, tall with several papery petals and lots of stamens round the ovary. Helena tipped some in her hand, then sprinkled them thinly over the ground. She did the same with an earthenware pot which she hoped would be a focal point at the end of the lawn, beside the arch. She really loved this time of year, creating a new and colourful garden where she and Bill could sit and relax with a glass of chilled dry white wine on some of those balmy summer evenings.

She busied herself for an hour or two, enjoying the feel of soil on her hands and dreaming of the warmer months. Then locking the shed and coming indoors, she glanced at the clock on the kitchen wall. Time for a shower before Bill was home, then all systems go for their evening meal.

The minutes ticked by and then the hours as Helena started to grow concerned. Bill was rarely home this late and usually rang when held up at work. She checked the phone – no missed call, no message or text about the delay. Why had he not contacted her? He knew she'd only start to worry. Why was he not answering his phone?

Helena sat and thought what he'd said before leaving

home for the office that day. Nothing unusual, it seemed to her, just the regular commentary as experienced every day of their lives – he hoped she'd have a really good day and he was looking forward to the evening already. Helena thought he meant with her but perhaps he didn't mean that at all. Perhaps he meant with somebody else. He'd certainly been a bit quiet of late, a bit distracted and overtired. She'd put that down to his busy job, to the usual office politics. She knew there had been another restructure, with colleagues in and colleagues out. Perhaps it was something to do with that.

Helena poured another drink and wondered what to have to eat. The fish lay in its pack unopened, so she opted for some bread and cheese. No point in struggling with the dreaded shrink-wrap, especially if she was dining alone.

Uncomfortable thoughts went around in her head as the night wore on and Bill never came. Perhaps he'd been injured or beaten up, but where and why and who was he with? This latter thought plagued her the most as she pictured the young office girls. Too flighty and frivolous by half and never dressed as office girls should, with their low-cut tops and skirts too short. It was never allowed in Helena's day and wouldn't be now if she was the boss!

How prim and old-fashioned she started to sound but these giggly girls could turn a man's head. Not her Bill, she'd previously thought, but now she wondered where he was and which of those floozies he was currently with.

It had to be one of them for sure, for where else could he possibly be?

Helena's mind was in a spin as she emptied the bottle of dry white wine. She didn't normally drink this much but at the moment it seemed to help (though it probably wouldn't in the morning). She picked up the phone and called Bill's friend, who only served to exacerbate matters by saying that Bill left the office at five with a red-haired girl draped over his arm. Or that's what Helena heard him say as she didn't wait to hear any more, flinging the phone across the floor.

Helena started to look for clues to her husband Bill's treachery. The seed that she'd earlier planted herself had taken root and started to spread. From the smallest of seeds, it grew and grew, out of control and taking her over. Innocent words were knocked out of shape, distorted and twisted beyond recognition, threatening to cause her lasting damage if she didn't halt this insanity soon. The green-eyed monster had done its work, manipulating her every thought, eating her up and spitting her out, clouding her judgment and rendering her mad. Everything now was out of proportion as Helena fed her perverted mind, picturing Bill in the arms of a redhead, no thought for his wife as she waited at home.

Eventually, she fell asleep but was woken up by a key in the door. She heard some movement in the other room, the fridge being opened, a drink being poured. She knew that this could only be Bill but was he alone or with a girl? He surely wouldn't bring someone back, not while she lay in their marital bed?

Cautiously, she crept to the door, holding her head that was throbbing now. Peering into the living room, she saw her husband all alone. He turned and held his arms out to her, caressing her with his gentle voice. How very glad he was to see her, to be home with his loving, adorable wife.

There'd been an accident at work. One of the girls had hit her head. Badly, on the metal shelf projecting from her office wall. Confused and bleeding, unable to stand, he'd practically carried her out of the door. In the commotion he'd left his phone, left his jacket and wallet behind. Bill had taken her to the hospital and stayed with her there till they'd patched her up. After that, he'd taken her home to her two flatmates who'd then taken charge. From there he'd walked back to his office where it was too late to call Helena up. He knew she'd already be asleep and knew that she would understand. But why was Helena looking so ill and why had she not cooked some tea? He sensed his day was about to get worse.

# TEARS OF A CLOWN

Wendy was talking to herself again. Out loud. It didn't matter when she was at home as no one heard her but out in the street people stared. She'd heard it said it was common in old people, especially when living alone, as they had no one else to talk to, but Wendy wasn't old. She was thirty-four. That's not to say she didn't feel old, because she did. Old. At thirty-four.

Her fellow passengers were looking at her now as she journeyed home on the bus. She didn't seem to be able to stop talking and didn't always know she was doing it until she caught them staring. Mothers moved their children away and there was a flurry of changing seats, as nobody sat near her for long, this mad woman, chatting to herself.

It wasn't a conversation she had, merely a few words here and there, spoken aloud as she thought of them. Observations, or tasks to be done, like hanging out the washing or making the bed. It was almost like writing them down, laying them out in stone to help her to remember them, an oral to-do list to be picked up later. Sometimes she even whispered her words, as if telling herself an intimate secret that no one else but her should know.

Wendy's secret was hers alone and one that few would ever have believed. When seen in a crowd or group situation, Wendy was different again. She was never particularly invited to gatherings, but she often seemed to be there. How, was anyone's guess. She just seemed to join things, and nobody seemed to mind.

People in fact were glad, pleased when they saw her there, as she brought a party to life, made it go with a bang. She always came on her own but was never *on* her own, as she moved about the room chatting to all and sundry. Wendy could be relied upon to talk to the ill at ease, to those that others found boring, to the shy and socially awkward. She gravitated towards them, made them feel at home, made them feel relaxed and a welcome part of a group. That was Wendy's skill – bringing everyone in, leaving nobody out.

If she asked how somebody was, she listened to the answer. She was genuinely concerned, truly wanted to know. So many asked the question but didn't hear the answer. Didn't *want* to hear the answer – it was just something to say, a standard opening line that required no response. It was very upsetting to say how you really felt, only to be ignored with a "that's good" reply. Wendy had known that herself, experienced it many times, but none of those around her would have ever really guessed. She was the life and soul of the party, everybody's friend, good to be around, the light in everyone's day.

That wasn't how Wendy saw it, as she travelled home alone. She wondered to herself how people found their friends. Good within a group, she was sad upon her own. Wendy often found it was hard to get through the day and watched the clock go round with every passing hour. She pounced upon her phone each time she heard it ping and kept it always by her side in case anyone cared to ring. It was a myth about her life that she'd somehow once created, that she was always busy with friends, but the reality for Wendy was really rather different. Being busy, of course, suggested a life full of purpose and, while she did indeed try to keep herself busy, it was usually on her own. At least it passed the time.

She'd joined so many groups to try and meet new friends but, despite the outward appearance, she remained a lonely figure. She enjoyed the drama group best, as she liked to be somebody else. She liked to don a mask, something to hide behind, so nobody would know her, know who she really was. She'd keep the myth going, of being somebody else, a strong character who made people laugh, while inside she was wanting to cry, cry at the farce of it all. She was a sham and only she knew it.

She thought of others who'd gone before her, of stars of stage and screen. It often seemed to follow a pattern. Some of the great comics of the world were very lonely figures and, in themselves, not happy at all. Such was Wendy Miller.

She sat on the bus and looked out, at the tears of rain running down the window that matched how she felt inside. "Tears of a clown" she said aloud, as if rehearsing her lines.

# A GAME OF SKITTLES

It had all looked so innocent that night in their local pub. Two small teams playing a skittles rubber, a popular game played for centuries in town and country alike, traditionally bringing communities together. And so it had been that Friday night in March, the folk of Lower Riding hosting a team from a neighbouring village. What could be more innocuous? What could be more enjoyable? A pint and a joke with some mates over a friendly game of skittles. Yet nothing was further from the truth, for within their midst there walked a killer who was ready to roll the ball.

Hannah stood with a glint in her eye behind the line at the start of the alley. Nine pins at the furthest end, a brand-new set bought by the club the previous week. Hannah knew she could knock them flat, all nine in one fell swoop, but that didn't fit with Hannah's plan, coldly calculated over weeks and months.

She bent and stared the length of the alley, fixing her eye on the front pin. She knew if she hit it with force and precision, she'd take out the front left quarter too. If her eye was in and her aim was steady, she could also manage the centre pin. Three down would be a result and would sit well with her deadly design.

The ball left her hand and rumbled down in a straight line towards its target. It cannoned into the first of the skittles, taking the other two as planned. Hannah allowed herself a smile as a scream went up from the other team and its young captain rushed from the room. All was chaos in the hall, chairs knocked flying, people running, sirens blaring in the street and the shouts of friends in frenzied alarm. Three members of a single family lost their lives in the village that night, faulty brakes on the car to blame.

The following week the skittles resumed, and Hannah was at the front again. Working out the exact trajectory, she kept her resolve as she rolled the ball, this time aiming for two together, the front right quarter and the winger behind. Down they went like dominoes, one falling against the other, as Hannah triumphed yet again. She acted surprised when she heard the news that two of the elderly in the village had both been struck by a passing van, one having stumbled off the kerb, grabbing the other to gain support. A figure had been seen running away and the driver had thought it had been a woman.

Hannah's turn came round again, and her eye was set on another three. Five down and four to go and she wanted to save the best till last.

She stepped forward, poising herself, carefully measuring the weight of the ball, happy to feel in full control. She knew the speed that was necessary, knew how to judge the line of her sight. The game was becoming easy now and Hannah knew she was up to the task.

The ball flew down the alley straight, heading for the three central pins. Down they went with a certain panache, never to rise up again. Hannah glanced across the room to where a group of revellers sat. They'd all had far too much to drink but three had more than they'd bargained for. It was easy to move amongst this crowd and swiftly pour the cyanide in. None had seen her move amongst them, as they laughed and chatted and downed their cocktails, but three would never drink again as one by one they slumped to the floor.

Back in the hall another week on, Hannah took up her usual place, waiting her turn and smiling within. The pool table was back in use and a round of darts was taking place in a separate room to the skittles match. Everyone seemed to be enjoying themselves, Hannah the most, as she sipped her champagne, pleased with how her plans had gone. She moved forward to take her turn, knowing she mustn't overcook it, as one pin only had to fall, the pin that would finally be the last.

Gently rolling the ball along, she watched as it hit the foremost pin, making it sway till it toppled over, narrowly missing the others around it. Just at that point a howl went up in the next-door room, followed by shouts and scraping of chairs. The darts match had gone horribly wrong as a flying barb had touched the board but landed on the dog below, making it yelp and cry in pain, as the poisoned tip did its work.

Hannah had knocked them down like skittles and couldn't resist a final flourish. Grabbing the nearest ball to hand, she flung it down to the waiting pins. All went down and then there were none.

Hannah walked through the crowded hall, taking her bottle of champagne with her, to be met outside by a uniformed man and the flashing blue light of a waiting car.

# THE HOMING PIGEON

It was there in the street. Just standing there. Danny thought it an ordinary pigeon at first. You know the type – one of the feral sort that used to frequent Trafalgar Square until it was forbidden by law to feed them. The sort that ate food from your hand and sat on your head. The sort that made a mess and caused you to slip on the pavement. Streetwise birds strutting their stuff in dull grey clothing.

Labelled by some as "rats with wings", for their potential to carry disease, they were sociable little creatures on the lookout for food. Tame little birds ready to chat – or coo as it's called in pigeon circles.

It made no attempt to fly away (Danny's bird, in the street before him), but such, he found, was often the case. How many times had he driven along, tooting his horn to scare one away, for it only to wait till the very last second before taking off and escaping death. Danny had seen one run over once and never forgot the dull, dead sound, as the poor wee thing met its end, feathers and bones in a ghastly mess, a flattened ball in the middle of the road.

Danny's pigeon didn't move but seemed to wink and

beckon him. He looked the pigeon in the eye as it winked again and tilted its head. Was it injured, Danny thought, or was it trying to tell him something?

It was then that he noticed the small glass tube attached to the pigeon's short little leg, with what seemed to be a scrap of paper inside. Danny approached the bird with caution, careful not to scare it away. It didn't appear to be afraid and was obviously used to being handled as Danny cradled it in his hands and took it through the house to his garden.

Gently placing it on the grass, he went to fetch his smallest cutter to score through the tube on the pigeon's leg and remove the piece of parchment within, without hurting the bird itself. He talked to the pigeon all the time, anxious to keep it still and calm. That done, he retrieved the script, written on fine tissue paper. MARRY ME, it simply said – nothing more, nothing less.

Danny smiled in puzzlement as the pigeon continued to wink at him, unperturbed at being handled or at the glass tube being cut from its leg. The message couldn't be for him, thought Danny as he read it again, but who was it for and who had sent it? Could the pigeon hold any further clues?

Danny was in his thirties now, a handsome young man who lived on his own. Married once, at an early age, his life had careered to a sudden halt when his beautiful wife had been taken from him in a freak accident in the Swiss Alps.

Admired by many a female eye – and male too, if they'd cared to admit it – Danny had stayed steadfastly loyal to the wife he'd won and lost in a year. His friends had wanted to see him move on, being sad and lonely on his own and the kindest guy you could hope to meet. They'd paired him up and arranged blind dates, but Danny had never followed through and carried on in his solitary state.

Looking down at the message again, he popped the parchment in his pocket, pondering on its direct words. He put some birdseed on the ground in front of his new feathered friend and brought a bowl of water out, enticing the bird to have a drink. The pigeon, he knew, must have an owner, for someone to have tied the message on but who and how and where and why were questions he currently couldn't answer. What to do with the pigeon now as it rested peacefully on the grass? Had it even completed its journey or was it taking a well-earned break? If it didn't have to find its own food, would it ever really want to move on? But who, thought Danny, was the mystery owner and who the intended recipient?

He'd heard before of messenger pigeons and their important role in the two World Wars, saving countless numbers of lives by delivering notes and cries for help. Their history went back further still, to the "ruler of rulers", Ramesses III, one of the great Egyptian pharaohs and early user of the pigeon post that warned of flooding along the Nile.

Closer to home were the pigeon fanciers, birdmen who kept and bred these beasts. It was these that Danny decided to approach about his own little messenger bird. They suggested he check for a ring on its leg, which he duly found with a number on. This would tell them the pigeon's home and, on his behalf, they sent it back.

By and by, it came again, a new message attached to its leg: I NEVER FORGET A FACE, it said, with a big red heart drawn beneath, a cupid's arrow passing through. He knew it to be the very same bird as he checked the ring number yet again. The owner expected an answer then and the pigeon this time was going to wait.

It sat on the grass, bobbing its head, surveying the scene from its wide field of vision, winking again from its side-mounted eyes and cooing softly at Danny's feet. How had it known where to come, to land again at this good man's house? What was Danny to make of it all? Had the pigeon got it wrong or had it indeed found its mark? He'd learnt of its very strong homing instinct, of its great navigational skills and speed but why choose him as its ultimate target? Why come to Danny's house at all?

How was Danny now to respond, to answer the notes that the pigeon had brought? He was, of course, more than intrigued to find himself on the end of it all. Flattered, yes, but was it a joke? A prank by one of his well-meaning friends? This homing pigeon held the key, if only Danny knew how to use it.

Danny approached the birdmen again, as he wanted to send a message back. He needed their help in attaching his note, as the little bird waited patiently, tilting its head and winking again. Only the pigeon knew the secret it carried, though the birdmen knew from whence it came. The address and town meant nothing to Danny, and he stayed in the dark, much as before.

All yours, read Danny's note that he tucked inside the little tube. He laughed at his own audacity, out of character but playing the game. That, he felt, was the last of it now. He'd never see the pigeon again.

Days went by and life resumed, to the way it had been before the pigeon came. Danny missed his little friend, its bobbing head and playful wink. He missed the notes the pigeon brought, the intrigue, mystery and puzzlement. He wondered where the pigeon was and if it had delivered his script. He hoped he hadn't been too bold in sending back a *billet-doux*.

But Cupid hadn't finished yet and sent the pigeon back again, this time in a carrier, held in the hands of a pretty lass. Danny gazed at the beauty before him, scarcely able to take it all in. "Hi, I'm Helen," the lady said, "and our pigeon has a message for you." Danny lifted it from its box and smiled as it winked in its usual way. He looked to see what the message said. Pigeons mate for life, it read, and he knew that was what he and Helen would do.

# SILENT NIGHT

Her mother had wanted to call her Anne. A nice, respectable English name with a few royal connections and after her own mother and grandmother, ensuring some continuity in the female line since they weren't the type of women who kept their own surname. Instead (and with no Spanish ancestry) her father had named her Soledad after a beautiful and mysterious woman played by Ava Gardner in *The Angel Wore Red*. A great beauty she may have been, but it was not to Soledad's credit that the character in question turned out to be a prostitute, however kindly portrayed. As a middle-aged, upright woman, this wasn't a profession she wished to be known for, however sympathetically she felt for those who had to tread that path. Ava Gardner could carry it off, being her own woman and the star of numerous other films, but Soledad was nothing like her and you know how people talk.

She had pondered changing her name. People did that these days. Deed poll it was called, although she didn't understand why. Something to do with legality, she assumed, although a deed was often a feat or some notable achievement. Contravening her father's wishes would certainly be that, she thought. Some of her friends liked her name for the way it sounded and because it was different. The Kates and Marys were even envious, although she'd have swapped with them any day, had she been able. She was reluctantly forced to admit that her name suited her in many ways. Summed her up nicely, in fact, if you could ignore Ava Gardner and her red dress. *Solitude*, it meant, or *loneliness*, very much the way she felt now. Very much the way she felt most nights, actually. She didn't understand how she had come to this or why she sat night after night a sad and lonely figure in a silent and empty house. Her life had been full in the past with a very busy job at the airport, run off her feet most days and constantly very stressed from dealing with a frustrated and demanding public, particularly when a flight was delayed. Heaven help her if one was ever cancelled!

Her life had changed mid-pandemic, with fewer people travelling and fewer planes taking off. So many jobs had been cut in the industry, hers included some months ago now. Age, she knew, counted against her, with less opportunity for the over-fifties. She had struggled to find a permanent job, accepting very short contracts here and there and a smattering of temporary work, none of which had remotely excited her. She felt herself on a downward spiral with nothing to do, nowhere to go and seemingly no prospects.

Solly, as colleagues had sometimes called her, anglicising her name to avoid a clumsy pronunciation, had suddenly ceased to exist. Within days of leaving her desk, she had somehow been forgotten, made into a nobody, cast aside like an old boot. Friends and colleagues had drifted away, rejecting her invitations to lunch and ultimately ceasing to reply at all. Callous, she thought them, shallow too, with no understanding of her new situation and no apparent wish to empathise. Their comments had been unkind and unnecessary, though their picture of her was, in part, true – nothing to offer in the way of chat, as all days were the same for her now, one relentlessly following the other in a ceaseless round of job applications. Not that it was her fault. It was just the way it was.

Sitting alone, in her savage wilderness, on a cold winter's night approaching Christmas, Soledad turned to the radio. A bit of music would surely soothe and cast away all gloomy thoughts. An unfortunate decision to switch on then, as the words of an old Fats Waller song, enjoyed by her in happier times, began to penetrate the room: *"No one to talk with, all by myself, no one to walk with, but I'm happy on the shelf."*[2] NOT happy on the shelf, Soledad thought to herself, not happy at all. It was far too long since she'd had a boyfriend and now it just exacerbated her loneliness. Soledad by name, Soledad by nature. This was her fate it seemed.

2  Fats Waller: "Ain't Misbehavin'"

She switched the radio off with a sigh and stared at the room around her. Another quiet night in, she thought. Just as well for she had no money these days, though she hankered after a wild night out. You could hear a pin drop in the room, if there was anyone there to drop it. Silence could be loud at times, screamingly so, and this was just such a night. She ought to be out partying, knocking back the wine and munching on crisps, but instead she sat, alone and miserable, ready for bed in her tartan pyjamas. It was only eight o'clock.

A rap on the door roused her from her stupor. A visitor, she thought, someone come to see her, to shake her from her lethargy and whisk her into the night. Hastening to put on her slippers, her bare feet finding their warmth, Solly leapt swiftly into action, tripping over the coffee table and bruising her ankle as she went. Her excitement numbed the pain as she unlocked the door, keys slow to cooperate as her fingers sought the hole.

Standing there before her, a group of neighbours' kids, glowing lanterns in gloved hands, dressed up for the Arctic in big woolly hats and thick knitted scarves tucked randomly into their navy duffels. On a count of three, the sweet-looking kids began to sing, their voices not as sweet as their looks, rather discordant and all out of tune. They were doing their best, she charitably supposed, but that was where her benevolence ended, so downcast was she at the vision before her, having moments before, in her mind's eye, seen a tall dark stranger or at least one she knew. Carols sung well she generally liked but carols inharmonious were different again and these were harsh on the ear indeed. Thanking them quickly to shut them up, Solly turned and closed the door, sinking to her knees in quiet despair, as "Gaudete" ended and "Silent Night" began.

Sobbing uncontrollably now, Solly stood up and looked in the mirror as the voices of the children tottered on outside. The face that looked back was alien to her, made worse by ragged strands of hair that clung to her cheeks from her big wet tears. Solly wondered what she'd become, crying piteously at how far she'd fallen, with the dreary prospect of her own silent night.

A Scrooge she was, full of misery and bile, on the cusp of a joyful Christian event, but still with time to turn this round and become the person she once had been.

Opening the door on the children once more, Solly clasped them in her arms, bringing them in and offering treats. Her silent night had turned into song, her sorrowful state into joy. Later that night, when lying in bed, carried away on the gentlest of dreams, Solly gave way to calm and contentment, having finally found her heavenly peace.

# SHORTS

The curtains were open in the pretty little bedroom at number 12 – just as Gertie had requested. They'd wanted to keep her in the dark, as they so often had towards the end of her life, both physically and metaphorically speaking. They thought it would trouble her, to know what was wrong, to know how much time she had left, but Gertie felt ready to meet her Maker, having simply and quietly made her peace. She only wished He would hurry up and get Saint Peter to open the gates, but who was she to make such a request. The Lord did everything in His own time and she just had to be patient with Him.

Her family stood around her like crows, all in black and sombre display. More like vultures, Gertie thought, knowing her will would be contested. There was nothing controversial in it, but the sons had never seen eye to eye and the daughters-in-law were at daggers drawn. Where did I go wrong, she wondered.

Gertie lay and looked out of the window, at the trees gently blowing in the breeze, at the swifts that flew over rolling hills *en route* to their summer breeding ground.

She doubted that *they* would have sibling problems or squabbles over the family silver. How graceful they looked as they raced on by, soaring high in a perfect blue sky. That would be Gertie before too long, free as the birds in celestial splendour and without a care in the world.

For now, she lay in her pink cotton nightie with daisies on the front and roses on the sleeves and drifted in and out of sleep. Images floated through her mind of when she was a little girl, curled up in bed next to her mum, safe and warm and happy inside. Her mum had read her stories each night, of kittens and bunnies and cuddly bears. She loved to hear these homely tales, however often she heard them read. If only her mum could read her one now, to give her comfort in her final hours.

Gertie lapsed back into sleep and dreamt of her childhood and sunny days, of happy holidays on the beach, of sandcastles, sea and ice-cream cornets. She pictured her dad building castles with moats, then waiting for the tide to come in, while her mum was the queen of the suntan lotion, lathering it on to their pale-skinned bodies clad in costumes or T-shirts and shorts.

Gertie called them her fun shorts and she thought them the best invention ever. Striped outside and striped within, the shorts were turned inside out when dirty, so providing a new clean pair, ready to play on the sand again.

Oh, that her life had been so simple, so easy to change from bad to good. If only her life could be turned inside out, to make it clean and fresh again.

Now awake, she pondered this, the dream of her shorts making her think. Nobody led a blameless life and Gertie was no exception to that, having twice been imprisoned for major fraud. If she could only but show her cleaner side, the dirty side might be overlooked.

She pictured her shorts on a washing line, being slowly caressed by a summer breeze. Dipped like cloots in a sacred well, then tied to a tree for the badness or illness to fade away, carried off by a healing wind.

Gertie had tried to show remorse for the crimes committed in her younger days but those she'd injured had never forgiven, including her family around her now, who stood as if forcefully egging her on to shed her mortal coil. She'd tried her best, on leaving prison, to make amends for what she'd done but her crimes for some had been too great, and Gertie was left floundering. Her past weighed heavy on her heart, and she continued to grieve for evermore. Until such time when she neared her end and thought she'd give the Lord a go. If she was after all to enter His house, she'd better tell Him how she felt and how she'd tried to atone for her life. She quietly whispered her words of prayer and felt that her God was listening.

Later that night, Gertie died, calmly and in a state of peace. Her family buried her the following week, dressed in her freshly laundered shorts.

Vida Cody was born and grew up in south east London where she still lives with Tia the cat. She took up writing in retirement and has never looked back.